"Wyatt, I can't...get involved."

"Then don't. Just kiss me now. No commitment and no promises."

"Just like before."

"No. Better. We're both adults. Let's see what it would be like for just this moment."

"Oh, Wyatt," she whispered. "Everyone always said you could sell ice to Eskimos."

He smiled, dipped his head and kissed her slowly. Very slowly, savoring her soft lips and warm mouth that tasted of hot chocolate.

"Toni," he whispered, but didn't know what else to say. No promises, he reminded himself. They weren't meant to be together forever, but maybe they were meant for each other now.

Dear Reader,

Happy holidays from my home in Texas to your place in the world. As I write this letter, I've just become a grandmother for the second time and I'm planning the last two books in my BRODY'S CROSSING series. The year stretches ahead, filled with promise and opportunities. I hope you feel the same during the Christmas season, regardless of which holidays you celebrate.

Both my hero and heroine have been mentioned in previous books and I just love both of them. Toni Casale is a strong career woman, beautiful and smart, doing well in a traditionally male occupation. Wyatt McCall is the type of man who has an insatiable zest for life, a high level of energy and enough boyish charm to make him the most popular man anywhere, even without his billions. Wyatt and Toni were an item all through high school, and everyone in Brody's Crossing expected them to be together forever. He had other ideas, leaving for college right after graduation, and leaving Toni with questions and no answers.

Now Wyatt is back in town, making good on a fifteen-year-old sentence by the municipal court, resolving his past transgressions so he'll be a good role model for the kids he's trying to help with his new foundation. And taking another chance on his relationship with the only woman he's ever loved. I hope you enjoy the time you spend with Wyatt, Toni and the rest of the Brody's Crossing citizens during this very special season. Best wishes for a wonderful holiday and a happy 2009.

Victoria Chancellor

A Texan Returns
VICTORIA CHANCELLOR

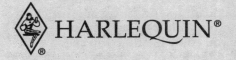

TORONTO • NEW YORK • LONDON
AMSTERDAM • PARIS • SYDNEY • HAMBURG
STOCKHOLM • ATHENS • TOKYO • MILAN • MADRID
PRAGUE • WARSAW • BUDAPEST • AUCKLAND

ISBN-13: 978-0-373-75243-0
ISBN-10:   0-373-75243-1

A TEXAN RETURNS

www.eHarlequin.com

Printed in U.S.A.

ABOUT THE AUTHOR

Victoria Chancellor married a visiting Texan in her home state of Kentucky thirty-five years ago, and has lived in the Lone Star State for thirty-two years, after a brief stay in Colorado. Her household includes her husband, four cats, a very spoiled miniature pinscher, an atrium full of tortoises, turtles and toads, and lots of visiting wild critters. Last year she was blessed with both a new son-in-law and a granddaughter. Her former careers include fine jewelry sales, military security and financial systems analysis. She would love to hear from you via her Web site, www.victoriachancellor.com, or P.O. Box 852125, Richardson, TX 75085-2125.

Books by Victoria Chancellor

HARLEQUIN AMERICAN ROMANCE

844—THE BACHELOR PROJECT
884—THE BEST BLIND DATE IN TEXAS
955—THE PRINCE'S COWBOY DOUBLE
959—THE PRINCE'S TEXAS BRIDE
992—THE C.E.O. & THE COOKIE QUEEN
1035—COMING HOME TO TEXAS
1098—DADDY LESSONS
1172—TEMPORARILY TEXAN*
1190—TEXAN FOR THE HOLIDAYS*
1215—AN HONORABLE TEXAN*

*Brody's Crossing

To my granddaughters, Lilly and Roxie.
Stay away from boys like Wild Wyatt McCall!

Chapter One

Monday, December 1, 2008

Wyatt McCall jammed his rented Hummer into Park in front of the Casale Remodeling offices. He stepped out of the vehicle and slammed the door. The sound was followed closely by the less forceful door-closing of his ever-present personal assistant's assistant, Cassie. On the other side of the H2, his public-relations director, Louisa, exited the rear passenger seat. "You might want to wait outside," he told the two women.

"No way," Cassie said, hugging her lightweight suit jacket around her. "You could need us."

"What, as witnesses to a murder?" he replied as he yanked open the front door. A large evergreen wreath adorned with a copper-colored wire mesh ribbon slapped against the glass inset and copper ribbons adorned with jingle bells jangled wildly as they bumped against the wooden door.

This building had been a small appliance store way back when he'd been a boy in Brody's Crossing. Now the walls, the flooring and the door looked different. More classy and modern. Efficient, not fussy. Toni had put her stamp on everything.

Including him. But that was very old news.

"Um, maybe you should wait just a minute to compose yourself," Louisa suggested.

"No way. I like my bad attitude." He pulled back his leather jacket to slip his Oakleys into the collar of his sweater. After looking around to get his bearings, he followed the hallway past an empty conference room to what appeared to be Toni's office.

"Hello, Wyatt," she said before he could get after her for ratting him out to a reporter about his youthful transgression. His last one in a long history of acts of misbehavior in Brody's Crossing.

She sat behind a modern design wood desk, her hands folded in front of her. By choice he'd only seen her a few times in the past fifteen years, on his rare visits to town, and always from a distance. She still took his breath away. Today she wore a royal-blue sweater and who-knew-what below. Jeans or chinos? A skirt that showed off her incredible legs? Or maybe tall black boots.

Her expression conveyed calm and serenity—the exact opposite of what he was feeling, now that he'd gotten his breath back. He wanted to ruffle her sleek blond hair. Pull her out of that big office chair and…

"I'm very sorry for what happened," Toni said. "When I spoke to that reporter, I only meant to give him background."

"Well, you did that," Wyatt said, stepping into the room. "Background that made me look like an irresponsible juvenile delinquent."

"Wyatt, in all fairness, you *were* irresponsible and a troublemaker."

He shrugged. "A minor infraction that you turned into a major incident." It was damned irritating that she'd revealed to the national magazine reporter, who was doing a story on Wyatt's newly formed foundation for at-risk kids, that he'd skipped town fifteen years ago, before finishing his municipal sentence for painting the water tower purple and gold. Once the story came out, questions from others in the media and even some business associates had elevated the old incident from a triviality into a potential problem.

How could a very successful man—albeit a former troublemaker—serve as a role model for potential juvenile delinquents when he'd been so irresponsible that he hadn't even completed his court-imposed sentence? He couldn't! He had to make this right so he could be a positive influence on those kids. He was one of the only people around who had both the money and the background to make a real difference.

His people had worked with the city officials to come up with a PR solution: Wyatt would come back to Brody's Crossing for some community service, to make amends for leaving the sentence unfinished, and he'd get photos and a new story on the importance of making things right. And personally he'd get to put his past misbehavior behind him. To make it right for himself, not just the town or the media.

Although at the moment, he could barely remember why he'd thought coming back to town was a good idea. Not with Toni Casale sitting in front of him, looking all serene and grown-up.

"You're not being very fair," she said.

"I'm not feeling very fair. As a matter of fact, I'm kind of angry." Angry at himself, for spending his youth as a prankster, and at her, for being mayor of the town in which they'd grown up. And at the situation, which was both their faults. He might have painted their school colors on the tower, but she'd leaked the news that he'd left town before it was completely boring-white again. Everyone in Brody's Crossing knew he'd left for Stanford fifteen years ago, white paint still under his nails, but only *she* had brought up the subject in an interview. Maybe, deep down inside, she was still mad at him for leaving so suddenly.

"I told you I'm sorry."

"Are you sorry as the mayor or as my former girlfriend?"

She drew in a deep breath. "Both, I suppose. Maybe because we used to be friends and I know what it feels like to be…disappointed."

He narrowed his eyes and suppressed a comeback. She had a point, one that he didn't want to explore at the moment. Her reasonable attitude and reminders of the past took the wind out of his sails. "Whatever your intentions, the point is that I'm back in town to finish my 'sentence' and we all have to make the best of it."

"With all due respect," Toni said, pushing out of her chair, "*I'm* not the one who has to do anything."

She wore a straight chino skirt, not as short as he'd hoped, with brown boots that looked more conservative than the stiletto-heeled black ones he'd envisioned. She hadn't gained weight in the past fifteen years. Not that he'd wanted her to, of course, but if she were sporting humongous saddlebags or if she'd started dressing like the construction workers she employed, he'd have had an easier time living in the same town with her for the next couple of weeks.

"You have to put up with me. It's hard to believe, but I can be hard to get along with. Just ask—" he turned, looking over his shoulder "—Louisa and Cassie."

He stepped aside and Toni peered around him. "Hello."

"Cassie McMann is my assistant's assistant and Louisa Palmer is my public-relations director."

"Hi," Cassie said, grimacing that characteristic funny smile of hers.

"Nice to meet you," Louisa said in her best PR voice.

Toni rounded the desk, grabbed Wyatt's arm and pulled him into the hallway. The fact that she'd gotten him alone almost made up for the defiant sparkle in her eyes. She dropped his bicep like a hot potato. "You brought your people to help you finish your sentence?" she asked in a raspy whisper.

"They're not here to help me do any actual work. I can handle that. They're here to keep me out of trouble with seemingly well-intentioned former friends. And the media."

"Would those be the *friends* you abruptly left when you

moved away? The friends you conveniently forgot to contact once you made it big?"

That sounded a bit personal. "I didn't forget the town." He'd sent checks to some of his parents' favorite causes. And maybe a few to make up for his youthful indiscretions. His foundation, based in California, would eventually work nationally to help kids who had gone astray and had no one else to pull them back from the edge. Bored kids, smart kids with too much time on their hands, frustrated kids. Kids from bad homes—or good homes where they weren't understood. The causes of their problems weren't as important to him as the result.

Some people might think he was just one more rich guy doing something to make himself look good, but this work hit a lot closer to home than most folks realized. He, more than most, understood the importance of channeling all that energy, resentment and anger into positive pursuits rather than lashing out at the most convenient target.

In his case, that damned water tower where he and Toni used to go to make out.

"You might not have forgotten that you grew up here, but you seemed to forget the *people* in the town," she said. "Your friends, in case you've forgotten."

"I didn't think that certain *friends* were interested in ever speaking to me again." He and Toni had had some outstanding arguments…and equally fantastic makeup sex. Except for that last time, when there'd been no makeup anything.

Toni rolled her eyes. "Come on, Wyatt. Bring your entourage and come over to city hall. I've arranged a meeting with the new chief of police and the city manager so we can go over the details of your 'sentence,' as you put it. You're lucky the city went along with your ideas about publicly making amends. They certainly didn't have to legally, since the incident happened fifteen years ago." She started back to her office.

Wyatt wasn't about to let that comment about an entourage go unchallenged. He put a hand on her arm, halting her. "Cassie and Louisa are employees, not an entourage."

Toni shook off his light grip as if she didn't want him to touch her. "I'm sure they're perfectly lovely women. I simply didn't realize what dealing with such a famous entrepreneur would entail." She walked to her desk and grabbed a big ring of keys. "Most people who come to visit don't bring their staff."

"I only brought two people," he said, then realized he sounded too defensive. "I'm still on the board of directors for my former business and I've got a foundation to get running."

"Believe me, I know. I've heard nothing but inquiries on the famous billionaire bachelor Wyatt McCall. I'm surprised you didn't bring bodyguards."

Cassie had suggested that very thing, but Wyatt didn't need them in Brody's Crossing. He wasn't exactly making news, he wasn't one of those "bad boys" who attracted paparazzi, and besides, staying in and around Brody's Crossing wasn't easy due to the lack of motel rooms. But he needed to get this task done so that the follow-up story would reflect well on his foundation.

"Being famous sure beats being infamous," he said.

"In your case," Toni said, looking back over her shoulder as she grabbed her own brown leather jacket on the way out the door, "I'm not sure there's a difference. At least, not here in Brody's Crossing."

"You'll know soon enough. I'm going to be on my best behavior." Despite the way Toni looked in that modest skirt and that beckoning blue sweater. She'd always had a figure made for sweaters. And short skirts.

"I sure hope so," she said. "For all our sakes, please just do the work to finish your sentence and get back to the West Coast."

"That's the plan, isn't it?" he said as he settled his sunglasses in place and followed her out the door. Of course, when had he ever followed someone else's plan?

THE STATUTE OF LIMITATIONS had run out long ago on the crime of painting the water tower purple and gold, but the memories of most people in town were vivid, Wyatt learned as he walked down the sidewalk along Main Street.

"Wyatt! Good to see you back. You stay out of trouble, now, you hear?" Rodney Bell called out from across the street.

"Wyatt, you devil. What are you up to now?" Bobbi Jean Maxwell asked with a big grin as she parked her car in front of the bank on the corner.

"Wyatt, what devilment do you have planned this time?" First National's president, George Russell, called out from the bank's entrance, chuckling and waving as Wyatt, Toni, Cassie and Louisa walked past. Good thing the citizens of Brody's Crossing only knew about a few of his misdeeds. The tip of the iceberg, so to speak.

They crossed Main Street and headed to the city administration building on the opposite corner. Hopefully, this meeting would be quick. He'd get his sentence and get this ordeal over with. He had no intention of doing anything to give the citizens of Brody's Crossing any new fodder for gossip. He was a changed man, an adult.

Well, most of the time, anyway.

He got his assignment from a rather apologetic city manager. Decorate the community center lawn for the holidays, using some existing decorations. In return, in Wyatt's honor, city officials were moving the annual chili dinner to the same weekend as the parade. They wanted him to make a few comments and attend the dinner, and then he was free to go back to California.

The new police chief—Daniel Montoya, according to the name tag and introduction—said very little. After all, this wasn't a police matter. This wasn't even a court matter any longer. As long as he didn't get into any more trouble, Wyatt and the police chief wouldn't have any reason to see each other except over a bowl of chili next weekend.

"That should give you some good opportunities for PR photos," Toni told Louisa, then looked at him as if it were *his* idea to play up his return to town. Hell, if it hadn't been for Toni blabbing to the reporter, no one would have known about the time long ago that he'd publicly shown his school spirit.

He agreed to the community center project, smiled and shook hands, then stalked back to the H2. He'd decorate the community center as it had never been decorated before. He'd show Toni Casale that he could be a model citizen, even when technically he didn't need to do a single thing.

"Buckle up," he told Cassie and Louisa as he pulled out of the parking space, heading around the block and back south toward their home for the next week or so.

"Do you have directions?" Cassie asked, glancing at the GPS installed in the H2.

"I know where we're going without satellite assistance," he told her. After all, he'd lived here for eighteen years. Although some new businesses had opened recently, most of the structures were the same, he noticed as they drove east on Main Street, just a couple of blocks from downtown.

Wyatt could have stayed with his parents, but since Cassie and Louisa were here also, he'd opted for the renovated Sweet Dreams Motel. The place looked much better now than he'd remembered from his youth, he thought as he pulled into the newly asphalted lot.

His parents had always referred to the place as "that rattrap" and made disparaging remarks about the people who stayed there. Transients and riffraff, they'd said. To Wyatt, the folks had looked more like hourly workers and poor visitors. Once, he'd ridden his bicycle over to see who was really there. He'd accidentally seen the former chief of police come out of one of the rooms, followed by a woman who wasn't his wife.

That had started Wyatt's brushes with the law. The old chief of police had never forgotten the nosy kid from the wealthiest family in town. The new chief, Montoya, seemed like an upstanding guy who wanted no part of the limelight. Smart man.

Wyatt parked between crisply painted white lines, then they went into the office. Before long they had their room keys and headed down the walkway that led to the ten or so doorways.

"So, your room looks comfortable," Wyatt commented as he deposited Louisa's suitcase in her room. She'd told him that each room was different. The one she'd chosen was sort of Hollywood glam, with old black-and-white movie-star photos and movie posters from the 1950s. The bedspread was silvery satin, the kind that you could imagine slipping off of at the worst possible time. A shiny aluminum Christmas tree sparkled with pink lights and black ornaments.

"My room is Old West," Cassie said, poking her head in the doorway. "It is soooo Texas."

Wyatt smiled. Neither of his employees had ever visited Texas before, so he doubted they knew much about what was authentic and what had been manufactured by Hollywood. He left Louisa's suitcase on her floor and walked next door to Cassie's room. Sure enough, there was knotty pine paneling, chunky wood furniture and an artificial pine Christmas tree with handcrafted ornaments. A vintage-looking red-and-black blanket covered the double bed.

"Were you a cowboy growing up?" Cassie asked, looking at a Remington reproduction print of cowboys racing after a stampede.

"No, not really, but I can ride a horse." Although his parents owned a ranch, Wyatt didn't know much about cattle. Most of his life, there had been more oil than cattle production on the acres. Plus, his parents had always said he was destined for bigger things than running a ranch.

He'd never thought that there was anything wrong with

running a ranch, although the idea of doing only that day after day made him itchy. He needed new challenges. He'd always been drawn to technology more than nature.

"I'd love to ride a horse while we're here," Cassie said. "I rode a pony when I was a child."

"That's all? You've never gone riding since then?"

"No." She grimaced again, and he couldn't tell if there was a good story or a bad one behind the single-word answer. He hadn't spent a lot of time around her, since she reported to Brian Peters, his jack-of-all-trades assistant. Brian was back in California, running interference between the new foundation director and Wyatt's continuing business interests. Cassie had seemed a good fit for the short trip to Texas because he needed someone to handle things that Brian usually tackled.

"We'll go out to the ranch. Or if my parents don't have horses you can ride, we'll visit someone who does. I know lots of people who still live around here."

"The horses won't be dangerous, will they?" Louisa asked, entering Cassie's room. "Getting hurt while we're here wouldn't be good press."

"I don't want to be any trouble," Cassie said.

"No, it will be fine. Nice. I haven't ridden lately, either."

"You're a fun boss," Cassie said.

Louisa nudged her. "Come on, let's get unpacked. I have a press release to prepare for the Web site and the local newspaper."

Wyatt left the women and walked a few more steps down the covered walkway to his room on the end. This was the honeymoon suite, the manager had told Cassie when she'd reserved the rooms. It was the largest suite and featured a whirlpool tub and walk-in shower. He unlocked the door and stepped onto thick gray carpet. A king-size bed with a pink-and-gray retro-print satin bedspread dominated the room. Two chairs in what he thought were Danish Modern style sat beneath the corner windows. On the table between the chairs there was a fluffy white Christmas tree with clear lights and glittery stars.

He rolled his suitcase to a stop near the bed, then placed his laptop case on the table. There was also a built-in unit that hid the television, a small refrigerator and microwave.

"For those late-night honeymoon snacks," he muttered on his way to the bathroom. Not that he knew from personal experience. He'd never been married or even come close. He'd been very careful to avoid that trap.

The bathroom was spacious and modern, tiled in pink and gray, as if it were really from the 1950s. The place would be fine for him. After all, he wouldn't be in town that long. Just long enough to decorate the community center, participate in a few local activities and see old friends whom, as Toni had pointed out, he'd neglected in the past fifteen years.

Hell, he'd been busy. He'd had a company to build, a product to develop, a fortune to amass.

Besides, they all had lives *here*. Families and friends and futures in Brody's Crossing. He'd run from Texas as fast and as far as he could. He'd spent the past fifteen years hugging the West Coast, literally. His house overlooked the Pacific and he ran on the beach now, as far west as possible without crossing the ocean.

"Hello?" A woman's voice pulled him from the bathroom and into the main room. He must have forgotten to close the door.

A statuesque pregnant blonde stood next to Cal Crawford. He'd gone to school with Cal's younger brother, Troy. Cal held a little boy, so he supposed the rancher was a family man now.

"Hey, Wyatt," Cal said. "Good to see you."

"Mr. McCall," the blonde said, holding out her hand, "I'm Christie Crawford, the owner of the motel. I just wanted to say hello and welcome you back."

"Thank you, Mrs. Crawford," Wyatt said, slipping back into "Texas mode" easier than he'd thought possible.

"Christie, please."

Wyatt smiled and nodded. "Christie, then." He reached forward and shook Cal's free hand. "Good to see you, Cal. Where's that brother of yours?"

Cal snorted. "New Hampshire. Married to a Yankee vegetarian organic farmer."

Wyatt laughed at Cal's description of his sister-in-law and his obvious scorn at the idea of Troy living in the north. "And who is this?"

"This is Peter," Cal told him. "He's fifteen months."

The baby smiled, showing several teeth, and struggled to get down. "He's a handful," Christie said.

"I suppose so." Wyatt knew nothing about babies, except that they eventually grew into children who needed computers and software and digital television. They wanted games, text messaging and media uploads. He was all for that, but as for the little ones still in diapers…he'd leave them to their parents. "So, you're a dad," he said unnecessarily to Cal.

Cal smiled—something Wyatt didn't remember him doing much when they were younger. "Married and everything, with another one on the way."

"Congratulations. Still on the Rocking C?"

"Of course. We're building a new house, so it's kind of torn up right now."

Wyatt nodded. He stayed away from construction whenever possible. Why be uncomfortable and inconvenienced like that? He'd bought his house empty, but completely finished after the former owner had gone belly-up in the import business.

"I'll let you get unpacked," Christie said. "Is there anything else you need? We have a conference room next to the office, and we keep coffee, drinks and snacks by the front desk."

"I'm just fine, thanks. I can run by Casale's Grocery if we need anything." And possibly see Mrs. Casale, who probably didn't want to see him. If only she knew what he and Toni had been doing all those nights when they'd told her they were studying. Exploring human anatomy was more like it.

"Just let me know if you need anything," Cal's wife said, and Wyatt promised he would as he shut the door after the happy couple.

What he needed was for this week to be over with, so he could put Brody's Crossing behind him…again. Louisa would get her PR photos, the magazines would have their stories and he'd get back to his real life. The one without a certain blonde who could play havoc with his peace of mind.

He'd return to his house, where his housekeeper, Mrs. Nakimoto, had no doubt contracted with a decorator or two to produce stunning Christmas trees for several rooms in his white-on-white house.

Not one of them would have vintage or handmade ornaments, like this motel fifty miles from anywhere. But they'd look good, at least to some decorator's critical eye.

He unclipped his cell phone from his waistband and fell back on the bed. Were there any decent channels on the TV? He wouldn't be too surprised to see old reruns of *I Love Lucy* or *Lassie* in this family-oriented community, although since he was in the honeymoon suite, perhaps they had something racier.

With Toni nearby he didn't need sexy movies to heat his blood. She'd starred in quite a few of his dreams over the years, even though he'd tried to get her out of his head. Now that he was back, he decided, reclining on a satin comforter, he'd have to work extra hard to stay angry at his former girlfriend.

The other option—that he give in to the attraction that hadn't ever gone away—wasn't a good alternative. Not if he wanted to be on his best behavior for the next week.

Chapter Two

Toni carefully pulled apart the blinds on her front window and looked at the wooded lot surrounding the community center across the street. Wyatt stood in the midst of white wire reindeer pieces, the kind wrapped in tiny clear lights. He appeared frustrated and a bit lost, hands on his hips, shaking his head. He probably hadn't assembled Christmas decorations in years, if ever.

The McCalls had always been the type to have tasteful pre-assembled decorations. They did not have a herd of white reindeer who bobbed their heads or tossed their antlers side to side. They had one evergreen wreath on their front door, which was surrounded by red lights twined in a garland with silver-and-gold balls. Very subtle and tasteful.

Wyatt wasn't subtle, although whenever she'd seen him in person or in a photo, he'd been dressed appropriately. Today he wore a weathered brown leather jacket and leg-hugging faded jeans with heavy work boots that she was surprised he owned. A brisk wind blew through his sun-streaked hair and gave ruddy color to his perpetual tan. He looked good. Too good for her peace of mind. She didn't want to think of Wyatt as her former boyfriend. That era was long past. He was here to do a job. She already had two jobs to do, as mayor and business owner. No, she was better off thinking of Wyatt only in terms of *now*.

Toni sipped her hot tea and wondered what type of holiday lawn decorations graced Wyatt's Carmel, California home. Something modern and stylish, if he had any decorations at all. He was, after all, a bachelor. From what she'd read, he traveled a lot. He still did daredevil stunts at times. He lived a fast, full life.

Her life wasn't fast, but it was certainly full. Busy. With the new projects going on in town—which she had certainly hoped and worked for—her remodeling company kept her on a demanding schedule. She'd come to the point where she had to make a decision about running for office again. There had been some talk, she'd been told, that a few people thought her two jobs overlapped too much.

She dropped the blinds and shook her head. She wouldn't think about that right now. Today was Tuesday and she had a city council meeting tonight. During the day she and her crew would be on the site of her first joint venture. She was converting the old hotel across from the train station into six condo units, with retail and public areas as well. The project was ambitious and exciting, funded by Christie Crawford with a little help from Toni's brother, Leo, who owned the local hardware store.

Toni looked out the window again just in time to see Wyatt throw a deer head to the ground. Oops. He was getting frustrated, and an unhappy Wyatt would not be good for Brody's Crossing or for himself personally—just in case anyone was watching or listening. She set her mug on the windowsill, grabbed her fleece jacket and ran out the door.

WYATT STARED AT THE REINDEER parts in disgust. A simple task had turned into a morning of frustration because someone hadn't kept the directions or the original boxes. The five reindeer had been disassembled and stored in a big discarded refrigerator box. He'd already spent an hour untangling their wire antlers from their spiky legs. If he hadn't promised the community center director that he'd use these specific reindeer, of which she was so proud, he'd chuck the whole lot in the Dumpster and buy some new ones at the Wal-Mart in Graham.

"Need help?"

He whipped around to see another object of his frustration—albeit from a very different source—stop on the other side of the reindeer pile. "Spying on me, Miss Mayor?"

He thought he saw some guilty color in her cheeks, but it might have just been the cool, damp wind whipping through the bare limbs of the cedar elms.

"No, but I did *notice* you working on the Christmas decorations," she replied, folding her arms across her chest.

Yep, she'd been spying on him.

"I'd be better off buying new reindeer and hiring a professional to put them together."

"That wouldn't be in the spirit of your return to Brody's Crossing, would it?"

"Maybe not technically, but it would be the fastest way to get the decorations up and running."

"Fast isn't always best."

"You've got that right, babe," he said with a big grin. Sure enough, he'd irritated her.

She rolled her pretty brown eyes and tightened her arms. "I thought you'd grown up in the last fifteen years."

"I've grown a little. Would you like to check me out?"

Toni threw up her hands in defeat. "I was going to offer to help, but now I'm going back to my house. You're impossible." She spun around and marched away.

"Hey, what about these reindeer? I could use some help."

"Get the instructions off the Internet," she shouted as she crossed the street. "I heard that you're a whiz at that online stuff."

Wyatt shook his head and chuckled. Toni might have grown up and he might have moved on, but they still had something buzzing between them, he thought as he went back to sorting reindeer parts. The question was, with such a short stay in Brody's Crossing, did he want to find out whether the buzz was a good one or if it might be bad for both of them?

WYATT ENTERED THE CAFÉ for lunch with Louisa and Cassie. He still wore his work clothes from the reindeer challenge, which he'd conquered at last. The small herd of critters were now bobbing and swaying away in the yard of the community center.

"I see an empty spot," Cassie said, guiding them down the aisle between the old-fashioned counter and stools and the red vinyl booths. Wyatt brought up the rear, taking time to look around at the people having lunch. He recognized a lot of them. Some didn't look any different, but a few of the men had lost their battles with baldness and one or two of the ladies had gained a few pounds since he'd last seen them.

"Why, Wyatt McCall," a plump middle-aged lady called out as they passed.

He took a moment to realize this was Clarissa Bryant, owner of the beauty shop on the main street in town. His mother didn't frequent her shop, saying it was a hotbed of gossip. Which meant she thought the ladies were talking about *her.*

"Hello, Mrs. Bryant. How are you?"

"I'm just fine. It's good to see you back in town."

"Glad to be back."

"Just in time for the holidays. I think we're going to have the best Christmas yet."

"I'm not sure how long I'll be staying, but I'll be here for the parade on Saturday for sure."

"I hope you can stay," she said with a sparkle in her eye, "but only if you keep yourself out of trouble." She nudged the lady next to her, also middle-aged but not as flamboyant.

"Venetia, do you remember when the Settlers' Stroll was attacked by wild Indians?" Mrs. Bryant asked the other lady.

"That was something to see," Venetia replied, "not that I'm looking forward to it again."

Wyatt smiled and shrugged. "You never know, but I suspect all the wild Indians in the region have been tamed."

The ladies laughed. "Wyatt, this is Venetia Williams, who works at my shop, and you remember Caroline Brody, of course."

"Yes, ma'am, I surely do," he said. She was the mother of his best friend in high school. "How are you, Mrs. Brody?"

"I'm doing just fine, Wyatt. Working part-time in James's law office."

"And how is Mr. Brody?"

"He's doing real well. He had a mild stroke and retired from the hard work, but he's keeping busy at the ranch. You should come out and see us. James lives over his office with his wife, Sandy, but it would be like old times if everyone could come out to the ranch."

"Yes, it would. I'll have to do that. I was going to see James later, or tomorrow maybe. The mayor's keeping me busy at the community center."

"We heard," Clarissa said, giving credence to his mother's claim that the beauty shop was the place to hear gossip. "Myra Hammer said you were busy putting up those lighted reindeer."

"Yes, ma'am. They're just about ready."

"Don't forget the lighted Christmas trees," Venetia reminded him. "You can't have the reindeer without the white trees."

"I'll be sure to ask about those," he replied. "If you'll excuse me, I'd better get to our booth before the ladies order without me."

"Good to see you, Wyatt," Mrs. Brody said.

As he walked away, he heard Venetia whisper, "Do you think one of those young ladies is his girlfriend?"

"Maybe both," Mrs. Bryant replied, and then they chuckled.

He should have introduced Cassie and Louisa, but they'd

already walked past when Mrs. Bryant spoke to him. Next time, though, he'd make sure everyone knew that they were employees. He didn't need rampant speculation that he'd brought two young women to town for his amusement while he completed his sentence. Besides, they were both professionals, even if Cassie looked as though she would be scared to death if someone whispered "boo," and Louisa was so petite a blue norther could blow her away.

"What's good here?" she asked as he sat down across from them.

He took another look at her thin face. "You really should try the cheese fries," he said with a smile and picked up a menu.

What a blast from the past. This place had barely changed. Even Mrs. Brody looked the same. She was the mother of his best friend from childhood through high school. He and James had been a pair, getting into more trouble than any of their parents could handle. Well, to be honest, Wyatt reminded himself, *he'd* gotten James into more trouble than the Brodys could handle. From the comments of the ladies in the booth and the people he'd already talked to on the street, everyone expected him to continue to get into trouble.

Well, this time he wasn't going to meet their expectations. Despite wanting to provoke Miss Mayor, he was going to be on his best behavior while in town. Decorating the community center for Christmas was a mild sentence, one he could work through as long as he didn't have to assemble many more mechanical displays. And he wouldn't be terrorizing the Settlers' Stroll or streaking past the church or painting the water tower. His old paraglider was long gone, as was his souped-up pickup truck. He was pretty sure his parents had gotten rid of the ATVs and dirt bikes, so really, how much trouble could he get into in one small town in only a week's time?

"YOU'VE HAD TWO CALLS FROM the national press, one from the *Graham Leader* and one from the Wichita Falls paper," Eileen Breslin told Toni as she entered the municipal building. "They all want an update on Wyatt's community service. And here's the report from last week's zoning commission meeting."

"Thanks," Toni said as she accepted the multiple pink message slips and a stapled report from the city government receptionist-secretary-information desk. Eileen could also fill in as the police dispatcher, serve on the volunteer fire department and substitute teach if she had to. In addition, she coached her eleven-year-old daughter's softball team. Toni always felt like a slacker around Eileen.

Toni walked down the hallway toward the mayor's office. It wasn't a very big space, since the day-to-day operations of the city were taken care of by the city manager. The mayor was part of the city council, voted on issues coming out of zoning and other departments, developed ideas for possible projects and performed ceremonial duties, mostly.

Ceremonial duties such as introducing Wyatt McCall at the chili dinner on Saturday at the community center. She'd say some nice things about him, he'd say some nice things about the town, and then he'd ride off into the sunset. Again.

She closed the door to the office, blocking out the soft Christmas music playing throughout the building, and spread the message slips in front of her. Everyone wanted to know what was going on with him. Not much, as far as she could tell. He had managed to assemble five reindeer, despite his earlier frustration. Then he'd taken a two-hour lunch. He was probably accustomed to such leisure pursuits, especially now that he was semiretired.

"Retired," she mumbled. Who retired at age thirty-three? Someone who could afford to, that's who. But even as she thought about the idea of unlimited leisure time, she knew she wouldn't retire even if she could. There was too much to do. Too many buildings to renovate, businesses to encourage, clients to work with. She didn't want to give that up, even if she could somehow magically afford to do so.

She enjoyed being a catalyst in the renewal of Brody's Crossing. Someone needed to take a lead role in bringing the town back, if not to railroad-oil-cattle-boom days, at least to a realistic standard. The zoning report was about the removal or renewal of dilapidated buildings, although she'd have to excuse herself from votes relating to her renovation projects.

She'd just finished her phone calls when Wyatt's press secretary—or perhaps she was a public-relations director—showed up.

"Hello, Louisa," Toni said, hoping she'd remembered the young woman's name correctly. "What can I do for you?"

"I was wondering if I needed a permit to take photos on the community center property or on a public street. I wanted to get some to update the foundation Web site and perhaps some video that could be used for downloads by the media."

"Technically, you need a permit, but since Wyatt is serving an unofficial sentence at the community center, there won't be any problem taking his photo. I can call the director for you and let her know you're coming by."

"Well, if you're sure. I wouldn't want to cause more trouble for him that would come back to haunt him later."

"You won't." Toni eyed the efficient-looking and -sounding PR person carefully. "You know, despite what Wyatt thinks, I didn't intentionally tell that reporter about him leaving town before he finished repainting the tower. It was an honest mistake."

"I'm sure that's between you and Mr. McCall."

"Yes, but you might think I'm looking for a way to make trouble for him, because that's what he thought at first. Perhaps he still does. I'm not trying to hurt his reputation or bring up the past. Believe me, I'd rather he only visited town to see his folks. His arrival here is causing quite a stir."

Louisa shrugged. "He's a draw wherever he goes."

"I'm sure that's true. We see photos of him at many high-profile events." People who felt that Toni might be interested in knowing what her former boyfriend was up to often showed her entertainment and business news stories and photos of him. She always smiled and said, "Isn't that nice," or some such remark, and went on with her day. If she ever showed the least bit of interest in him, someone might interpret that as an "attraction," which she could never acknowledge. Her feelings for Wyatt were absolutely private.

"If you'd be more comfortable, we can rush through a permit. However, I'll be glad to make that call and you can take your photos whenever the light is right or Wyatt starts working again."

"Oh, he's there now. We had lunch—a working lunch, actually—and then he went back to the community center."

"That's fine. I'm not keeping track of him that closely. As I said, I just want him to finish his task and then Brody's Crossing will get on with Christmas."

"He's doing his best. He's serious about this foundation. I'm sure he's anxious to get back to California."

I sure hope so. He definitely wouldn't be leaving before the chili dinner on Saturday evening, though. "Please, let me know if you need anything else," she told Louisa, hoping the woman would take the hint and leave so they wouldn't have to keep talking about Wyatt. If there was one thing that could spoil her holiday spirit, it was constant reminders that she'd been dumped by her now-billionaire boyfriend.

AFTER WORKING AT THE COMMUNITY center for another few hours, setting up white spiral Christmas trees and big lighted boxes trimmed with bows, Wyatt decided to call it a day. He needed to go see his parents. They'd wanted him to come out last night, but he'd put them off. He'd needed to get settled, he'd told them, which apparently had sounded reasonable. Tonight, he had no excuse. With a sigh, he plugged in the extension cords and watched the Christmas display light up the cloudy afternoon. Everything seemed to be working properly.

He looked across the street at Toni's neat cottage-style house. The frame siding and roof looked new, or at least well kept. She'd come out just a little earlier and swept the porch and walkway, looking at him occasionally. He knew because he'd been looking at her. She'd finished in what was probably record time and retreated inside. She hadn't spoken to him since this morning.

He rattled her. Good. She'd rattled him yesterday, with her calm demeanor and classic beauty. She'd grown into a woman in the years he'd been gone, but she still had a bit of the spunky girl he'd known—and at one time, loved—inside.

Good thing they hadn't stayed together, he thought as he gathered up the few tools he'd used. Or gotten married, which was where they were headed if he hadn't left town when he had. Marriage would have ruined their relationship a little more slowly than his abrupt departure, but just as surely.

No, he'd done the right thing in leaving for Stanford as soon as he graduated from B.C.H.S. He knew Toni didn't understand, but better she thought he was a jerk than begin thinking about "the future." That place defined by white wedding gowns, giggling bridesmaids, two-point-three adorable children and a three-bedroom house near Mom and Dad. The reality was more like credit card bills, snotty noses, dirty diapers and family feuds.

He'd actually done Toni a favor by running off, he thought as he placed the tool kit inside the community center storage closet. She'd gone to college not so far from home, started her own business and been elected Brody's Crossing's first female mayor since the early 1900s. Back then, the widow of a popular but crooked mayor who'd been shot in front of what was now the Burger Barn had taken over her husband's position. Life was considerably more civilized now.

Wyatt stretched the kinks from his back and walked to the Hummer. He pulled his cell phone from his jacket and called his parents. There had been a time when calling in advance was absolutely essential. Now, it was more of a courtesy.

"Hey, Mom. I'm headed your way. Can I bring anything?" And by that, he meant from the grocery, but he didn't make any snarky comments like he used to when he was younger and his mother went to Graham or farther to get what she really wanted.

"A half gallon of milk," he repeated back to her. "Anything else?"

"No, we're fine," she answered.

"I'll be there soon." With another sigh, Wyatt slid behind the wheel. He shouldn't have asked. Now he'd have to stop by Casale's Grocery, unless he wanted to go way out of his way to the minimart at the gas station outside of town. Hopefully, he wouldn't see Mrs. Casale. He assumed she still didn't like him much. Good thing she'd never be his mother-in-law. Talk about awkward situations!

As soon as he entered the grocery store, he felt as if everyone was watching him. And they were. He was the only man around. There were mothers with school-age children and grandmothers and pregnant ladies. He recognized a few of the older women as he headed through the produce section toward the dairy case.

"Wyatt McCall! Why, I'd heard you were back. What are you up to this time?"

"Just setting up some Christmas decorations at the community center. How are you, Mrs. Hammer?"

"I've got arthritis in my knees and I just got over a nasty

sinus infection. Why are you setting up those decorations? You could hire someone to do that."

Leave it to Bud Hammer's wife to get straight to the point. He remembered Bud and Myra as being very contentious. "You know, I did a lot of crazy things when I was younger. It's time that I did something nice for Brody's Crossing, don't you think?"

"Well, that might be true, but I don't think setting up that yard art really cuts it. I heard you had more money than Bill Gates."

Wyatt laughed. "Hardly. But I do have enough to get by."

Mrs. Hammer snorted. "That's why you're putting up those plastic reindeer from Wal-Mart. Doesn't make a lick of sense to me." She shook her head and put a bag of bargain-priced bananas into her cart. "Just don't you mess up the chili supper, Wyatt McCall. That's a tradition."

"I'm looking forward to having a nice dinner. I promise I won't talk too long, either. Now, I need to get some milk for my mother. You take care, Mrs. Hammer."

"Oh, I will. You tell you parents hello for me and don't forget—behave yourself, young man."

Wyatt chuckled as he strode quickly to the dairy case. Young man. He was thirty-three, not eighteen. But some folks wouldn't acknowledge that, he knew. Some folks wouldn't forget his past. He'd thought he could quickly make amends by fulfilling the sentence the city had decided upon, but maybe it wasn't enough. The fact that he really was doing the work himself hadn't impressed Myra Hammer, so maybe it wouldn't fly with the rest of the town, either.

When had he become so concerned about what others thought of him? And was he cheap? Were people expecting better decorations? The community center director and city officials had specifically said he had to use the reindeer, trees and boxes they already had.

How could something so simple become so complicated?

He'd been back in his hometown for two days and his thinking had already been challenged by a little old lady. A cranky little old lady, at that.

He did manage to get through the checkout line without seeing Mrs. Casale or anyone else who had an opinion of his visit home or advice on behaving himself. The short drive to his parents' place—it wasn't really a ranch anymore, since they didn't raise horses or cattle—didn't take long. He passed a few of the "nodding donkey" oil pumps that dotted the landscape. His dad loved it when oil went over ninety dollars a barrel.

The sun was setting as he pulled to a stop in the parking area behind his parents' garage, and he sat for a moment admiring the oranges, pinks and purples of the sky over the low western hills. Texas did have some spectacular sunsets, but nothing rivaled the view from his wraparound deck at home when the sun sank into the Pacific. Sometimes he sat there in a teak deck chair, watching the sunset with his only housemate, Tiger, a ragged-ear yellow tabby who used to be a tomcat. The cat was as rough and ugly as the house was sleek and beautiful, but for some reason he hung around. Probably because Wyatt was the only person stupid enough to feed and care for him in a posh hilltop community that valued pedigree over the ability to catch mice.

Wyatt would be back in Carmel soon. Whatever decorations Mrs. Nakimoto put up were fine with him. He didn't entertain at home. Usually, he took a few friends—or perhaps a special lady friend—on a vacation at Christmas.

Putting up the "yard art," as Mrs. Hammer called it, at the community center in Brody's Crossing had made him think of all the holiday functions he'd attended—and then gotten into trouble over messing with the joy of others as they pursued their own Christmas traditions. The holidays weren't so much fun anymore, even though his options now were practically limitless and his mischief more expensive and polished.

"Hell, you're not a kid," he murmured to himself. It didn't matter how the older generation treated him. But what did he expect? To return to the days when he'd been bored, rebellious and overindulged? No way. He was an adult. He did what adults did. Well, adults with millions of dollars of discretionary income, he thought as he grabbed the milk and walked toward the home in which he'd grown up. The house had an addition, a new roof to accommodate the raised ceilings his mother had always wanted and a new flagstone entry and circular drive out front.

"Hey, Mom," he said, closing the back door behind him. He sat the plastic jug on the counter and lowered his cheek for a perfunctory and somewhat awkward dry peck. She was trying to be a good mother, he knew. About fifteen years too late, but maybe better late than never. At least she only smelled of expensive perfume now, not that vodka had much of an odor.

"Thank you for bringing milk. It's such a hassle to go to town for one item."

Maybe, but what else did she have to do in a typical day? "Where's Dad?"

"Watching one of those old television shows in the family room, probably."

"Do you need any help?" He hoped not. He hated helping his mother in the kitchen. He never knew where anything was, especially after the remodeling, and he set the table wrong every time.

"No, thank you. I'll let you know when dinner is ready. Lupe fixed us a roasted chicken and vegetables earlier, before she left for the day."

Oh, good. At least his mother wasn't trying to cook again. She had an uncanny ability to ruin any type of meat and burn potatoes until the entire house reeked. Lupe had been their housekeeper for several years now, and his mother actually seemed to like her. He remembered a time when his mother had found fault with everyone and everything. Except him. He'd always been her golden boy, even when he didn't deserve her support.

Wyatt sat next to his dad in a matching recliner and watched a rerun of a rerun of an ancient Western horse opera. His dad turned down the volume so it was barely audible, just enough to be irritating as he talked about the possibility of shrinking crop subsidies and lower oil prices now that the general election was history. Wyatt wished he had a beer as he waited to be called to dinner, but there were no beers in the fridge. Not any more. He felt the urge to do something outrageous, just to relieve the tension. That's how he'd gotten in so much trouble when he was a kid. Hell, he still got into trouble sometimes when he was bored. Maybe he hadn't grown up much at all, despite fifteen years and unbelievable success.

Then he remembered Cassie's request, and asked, "Do you have any horses here?"

"Not these days. They're too much trouble."

"My assistant wants to ride. I'll call the Brodys to see if they have any gentle mounts. I don't want her thrown or spooked. She's only ridden once, as a child."

"Is she your girlfriend?"

"No, Dad. She's my assistant. Purely professional." His dad had a hard time accepting the idea of women in career positions. He assumed women were only looking for boyfriends or husbands.

"Dinner's ready," his mother finally announced, and Wyatt practically launched himself from the recliner.

They ate in polite silence interspersed with polite conversation. He even used his best table manners.

"I'm planning a welcome-home dinner party for you on Thursday night," his mother announced just before dessert. "I was sure you didn't have anything planned."

"Mom, you shouldn't have. That's too much trouble. I

doubt anyone will want to come to a party on a weeknight." Him, especially.

"No, I checked, and everyone is delighted. And we can't have it on the weekend. Almost everyone will be busy Friday night with last-minute preparations for the parade on Saturday afternoon."

"How many people are coming to this party?"

"I believe we have nineteen acceptances and two maybes, so it's just a small get-together. Just a buffet dinner and dessert to welcome you home."

"Okay," he said, trying not to sound petulant as he stacked dishes to carry into the kitchen. "Mostly your friends, right?"

"Actually, I've invited some of your friends, also. James Brody and his wife, Sandy. She's new to town. Cal Crawford and his wife, Christie, who owns the motel as you probably know. Cal received a Purple Heart for his service in Afghanistan. He's a little older than you, but you remember him from high school, right?"

"Yes." Wyatt paused at the doorway to the kitchen. "Anyone else?"

"Why, yes. I've asked our mayor, of course. Toni Casale." His mother raised her penciled brows as she lifted the cover from a crystal cake plate. "She's still single, you know."

Wyatt forced a completely neutral expression. "You don't say." He turned and walked into the kitchen. Having a bunch of his parents' friends was pretty bad; having some of his own friends would make the night more bearable. Having Toni in his boyhood home... That was something else entirely.

He wondered if his mother had ever found out what he and Toni had done in his old bedroom. In the family room. In the barn. In his truck.

On that highly polished cherry table in the dining room.

As he placed dishes in the sink, he wondered if Toni would remember. If she'd be able to sit there and nibble on finger food at the table where he'd nibbled on her. The thought brought a smile to his face.

"You're grinning," his mother said as she entered the kitchen. She opened the refrigerator and took out a can of whipped cream.

"Oh, yeah," he said, other fond memories surfacing before he told himself to behave. "I'm just looking forward to your party."

"*Your* party," his mother corrected.

"One can only hope," he replied, eyeing the whipped cream and thinking of Thursday night.

Chapter Three

On Wednesday Toni began demolition on the old hotel. She met her crew, her brother and a glowing Christie Crawford at eight o'clock in the morning. Christie brought French vanilla coffee for everyone; Toni brought safety goggles and sledgehammers.

"Always wear your goggles, and if you're tearing out Sheetrock, ceiling tiles or anything with insulation, you need a mask," she told her two partners.

"Is there asbestos?" Leo asked.

"Thankfully, no. I got the environmental results back Monday." Right before Wyatt McCall had breezed back into town. "We're free to begin."

She wouldn't have scheduled everyone to be here if it wasn't safe, but Leo was new to the remodeling side of the business and he didn't know that. After he bought the hardware store, he'd become more familiar with fixtures, nuts and bolts, nails, screws and nice, clean tools.

"We're saving these front doors. I've marked everything else that is to be saved with orange tape. Don't damage anything that's marked. Other than that, you're free to tear out the cabinets and fixtures in the kitchen, the half wall, the 1970s paneling and those incredibly ugly aluminum wall sconces."

"Sounds great!" Christie said, hefting her sledgehammer. The polished, pregnant, blond former socialite marched with determination toward a half-wall addition covered in faux walnut. "May I take out the whole thing?"

"You're welcome to try," Toni said.

Leo laughed and headed for the kitchen.

Toni smiled at their enthusiasm and motioned for her professional crew to come in and begin the real work. Outside, a thirty-cubic-yard roll-off container waited for all the material that couldn't be reused or recycled. Her crew would sort wood, metal and drywall later, after the amateurs got tired of demo. Toni predicted it wouldn't take long.

Sure enough, ten minutes later Christie called it quits. A few minutes after she left, Leo said he really needed to get to the hardware store. He was perspiring and breathing hard. Toni wasn't sure what type of damage he'd done in the kitchen, but hopefully nothing too costly. She'd heard a lot of swings of his hammer, a little bit of swearing and repeated crashes.

As Leo removed his safety goggles and used a towel to clean off the dust, a person Toni had never expected here walked through the door. She moved behind the scaffolding her crew had just assembled and watched Wyatt look around, then step carefully through the dusty debris. He looked too good in his faded jeans, work boots, waffle-knit Henley and blue, plaid flannel shirt. No one would guess he was a billionaire high-tech entrepreneur. Correction—a retired billionaire. As if one could retire from being too rich.

"Hey, Leo," Wyatt said as he folded his sunglasses and placed them in the placket of his partially unbuttoned Henley. Toni had always found those shirts sexy, especially on a man with a nice chest and flat abs. Unfortunately, that included Wyatt, now more than ever since he'd grown up. "What's up?"

"First day of demo. Toni let us—Christie and me, that is— start the tear-out."

"Free labor, hmm?"

Toni felt a rush of heat. So now he was calling her cheap?

"Expensive labor, if they mess up," she said, stepping out from behind the scaffolding.

"Oh, look who's here," Wyatt said with a devious smile.

Toni glared at him. He'd known she was there all the time. He'd made that comment to bait her. And, yes, she'd taken the hook like a hungry trout. She wanted to kick herself, but she'd rather kick her former boyfriend for showing up on *her* job site and aggravating her on what was otherwise a very happy day.

She'd looked forward to getting the old eyesore of a hotel renovated for years, and now *she* was the person making the changes. She'd pulled together the team and shown Christie the possibilities that could happen with a little money and a lot of work. Leo had leaped at the opportunity to get into the renovation side of the business.

And then Wild Wyatt McCall had to show up.

"So, you're remodeling the old hotel. That's good."

"I'm glad you approve. Now, we should get back to work."

"Don't pay any attention to me. I'm just curious about what you're doing."

"*We're* doing *our* job, which is more than I can say for you at the moment." Toni stalked closer to where Wyatt stood by Leo and glared at her former boyfriend. "Why aren't you at the community center?"

"Well," he said, leaning his butt against the heavy old check-in desk that Toni was salvaging, "I was on my way over there, but it was kind of cold so I went to the café instead. While I was having my coffee and a cinnamon roll, I saw James Brody. He told me about the big news. A lot of people are looking forward to the old hotel getting remodeled."

"Most people don't like to see empty buildings around town, and especially something with this much potential," Leo said. "I'm glad we could buy it and make something useful."

"I was going to ask about that," Wyatt said. He turned to Toni. "What are you doing with the old place?"

"Condos, retail and restaurant space," Leo answered.

Toni glared at her little brother for answering for her. "And we really need to get to work," she said. Again, in case Leo or her crew had forgotten why they were here.

"Don't mind me. I'd just like to look around. I've never seen the inside of the old hotel. The passenger railroad stopped running before I can remember."

"You're not looking around without proper safety equipment. If you want a tour, we have to fit you with a safety helmet and goggles. I might even make you wear a mask. Who knows what you'll find in the dust and debris? There might even be the hantavirus from years of mice infestation."

Wyatt shuddered. "That's just cruel."

Toni smiled, which she suspected looked a bit evil at this point. Wyatt hated mice. He'd play with snakes and let tarantulas crawl up his arm, but show him a little mouse and he'd freak like a baby.

"Okay, I can take a hint. I'll leave. I don't want to keep you from your work."

"I'm glad you stopped by," Leo said with his friendly grin.

"I'm sure your sister is glad I'm leaving," Wyatt said.

"Hello? I'm right here."

"So you are. And I'm outta here." Wyatt saluted them with his thermal coffee cup and turned on his heel.

"Come back when my sister isn't here and I'll give you a tour," Leo offered.

Wyatt paused at the tall double doors. "Now, that wouldn't be as much fun, would it?" he asked with a smile.

Toni punched her brother in the arm as soon as Wyatt sauntered away.

"Ouch!"

"Stop being nice to him. He needs to stay focused on his task, get finished and get out of town."

"Why? He's got a right to visit Brody's Crossing."

"He can visit his parents. He doesn't need to visit our job site." As a matter of fact, he didn't need to show up anywhere that Toni might be, as far as she was concerned. He could simply have his assistant or his PR person contact the mayor's office when the community center was finished.

The sooner, the better. The Christmas parade was this Saturday, followed by the chili dinner, and then the events started happening really fast. The holiday would be over before they knew it. Toni didn't want the whole season ruined by Wyatt's jabs and innuendos.

"I'm getting the crew in here to finish the demo. The faster we get this started, the faster we'll be finished and on our way to a nice profit."

"I'm all for that," Leo said. "I'll get out of your way."

Toni hoped that everyone would stay out of her way. Especially annoying eligible bachelors who thought they were just too funny.

"Just a few more days," she told herself as Leo left for the hardware store and the crew got started undoing years of bad decorating and poor maintenance.

And then she remembered that she had to attend the McCalls' dinner party tomorrow night. And see Wild Wyatt again. And if she knew his mother, who was a stickler for boy-girl-boy-girl protocol, she'd probably have to sit next to Wyatt at their dining table.

She wasn't ready for social engagements with him. There was no telling what he would do or say, and heaven help her, she seemed to have little restraint when it came to her responses.

But, she had one and a half days to get herself ready. Mentally and physically. She'd need every minute.

WYATT LOOKED AT HIS PITIFUL display of lighted figures in disgust. He'd driven by last night, after dinner at his parents' house, to see the reindeer, Christmas trees and gifts at night.

They looked terrible. He hadn't arranged them well, and they looked lost in the big yard surrounding the community center. There were lots of trees on the property, and they distorted rather than enhanced the scene of reindeer in the forest.

Not that lighted white reindeer in any way looked natural. Not to mention the spiral lighted artificial Christmas trees. Especially not now, in the light of day, in the clarity of the afternoon.

Darn it, Myra Hammer was right.

Wyatt sighed. He'd hoped his sentence would produce something worthwhile for the citizens of Brody's Crossing, but they couldn't possibly like this mess. He wasn't artistic. His creativity came out in user-based communications, with a strong emphasis on the "wow" factor. He could visualize new applications for existing technology, but bobbing reindeer had him totally baffled.

"I need help. I need a professional," he said to Cassie.

"What do you mean? They're all lighted."

"I don't mean an electrician. I mean a designer. A person who specializes in holiday displays, like maybe at malls or public facilities."

"I'll call someone. Do you have any ideas for local contacts?"

"No." He hadn't lived here in fifteen years, and even when he did live here, he hadn't been concerned with the design of Christmas displays. Unless, of course, there was a way to mess them up. Now, he had people who did this sort of thing at his corporate headquarters.

"Call my mother, and if she can't help call the mayor. And if that doesn't work, call a display company in Dallas or Fort Worth and ask them to get out here and put something up that will have a real wow factor."

"Any idea on budget?"

"I don't care. Whatever it takes. I want people to see this display and feel as if they're looking at Macy's windows in

New York City. Or one of those gaudy light shows at private homes that I've seen on television."

"Major store windows are started a year in advance, and those people who put up lights all over their homes begin in October at the latest." Cassie smiled crookedly and shrugged. "I watch a lot of decorating shows on TV."

"All I know is that with enough people and money, we can get this done by Saturday."

"It's already Wednesday!"

"Okay, get on the phone." He paused a moment, then said, "On second thought, you call my mother and the display companies in Dallas or Fort Worth. I'll go see the mayor."

"Um, I can call her, too."

"I know, but—" He stopped and narrowed his eyes at Cassie. "Why don't you want me seeing the mayor?"

Cassie looked down at her PDA. "Oh, she just doesn't seem to like you much, and I thought perhaps she'd be more helpful if I called her."

Wyatt scoffed. "She just thinks she doesn't like me."

Cassie frowned. "What's the difference? Either way, she might not cooperate."

"She'll cooperate. You forget the McCall charm factor."

"I'm not sure it's working on her."

"Oh, it's working." She wouldn't be so testy around him if it wasn't working. The high points of his trip so far had all involved getting Toni riled up. And he didn't even feel guilty. She wouldn't admit it, but she was enjoying herself. She was actually living. According to everyone he'd asked—discreetly, of course—Toni didn't have much of a personal life. She wasn't dating. She devoted all her time and energy to her business and her public responsibilities. And she did a damn fine job of both.

Still, she needed a personal life. At least for a little while. He'd be gone soon and she could go back to being Miss Conscientious. A little verbal sparring with a bad-boy former boy-friend wasn't going to ruin her work ethic.

"Well, you're the boss," Cassie finally said.

"Exactly," Wyatt said with a grin, looking at the reindeer. *Your days are numbered,* he told them silently, and headed for his Hummer.

"WE CAN'T POSSIBLY GET RID of the reindeer," Toni told Wyatt as he sat in her office. She was still dusty and tired from this morning's tear-out at the hotel, which her crew was continuing to work on. She'd taken out some of her aggression and frustration on a rickety banister leading to the second floor, but the physical labor hadn't helped much. Once again faced with Wyatt McCall, she wanted him out of her life.

Not so much wanted as needed, she corrected herself. He brought too much…turmoil. Yes, that was the word for Wyatt. Tumultuous. Wild and unpredictable.

She liked predictable. She needed order. "Why would you want to get rid of perfectly good Christmas decorations?"

"Why? Because they're not enough. They're not very convincing, as far as Christmas displays go. Wouldn't you rather have something really spectacular?"

"It doesn't matter what you or I want. Those decorations were a gift from the local Scout troops. They got together, raised money and presented the reindeer and trees to the city. If we toss them out, it will be a personal affront to every Scout and every family who participated in the bake sales and car washes that earned money for their generous purchase."

She watched a range of emotions move across Wyatt's face. He wasn't the most expressive person she knew. He usually kept his face in a steady mildly pleasant or devilish mode. Rarely did anyone know when he was genuinely angry or concerned. At least, the Wyatt she'd known fifteen years ago was that way, and she suspected he hadn't changed all that much.

Right now, he appeared frustrated.

"You're right. We can't diss the Scouts."

"*We* aren't considering dissing the Scouts. *You're* the one who doesn't like the decorations. I never realized that you were such a holiday design…enthusiast."

"You make that sound like something bad. Or tawdry." He shook his head. "I'm not an expert on design. That's why I want to hire someone to help make the community center really fantastic. You may not realize it, but I care about this town."

Toni shrugged. "You may care, but you don't spend much time here."

"My parents come to visit me in California. They enjoy the travel, and I have been a little busy with my business."

"And your social activities," Toni added, feeling somewhat testy as she remembered all the photos she'd seen of Wyatt attending this big function or that one, with a gorgeous woman on his arm or gazing adoringly at him.

"Jealous?"

"Don't flatter yourself. I'm just commenting that you had plenty of time to run around Hollywood or Seattle or New York City, but you've barely visited your hometown since you left. The hometown that you care so much about that you want to hire a design firm to install new decorations at the community center *you're* supposed to be fixing up for the holidays."

"I think you're jealous."

She pushed herself out of her chair so fast she almost gave herself whiplash. "I am not jealous! I'm… I'm angry."

"Why are you angry at me? For having fun? For having money to spend on the community center if I want to?"

She felt as if her head might explode. Arguing with Wyatt had always affected her this way. "Yes! I scrape every dime out of our town's budget, haggle with our city manager for needed projects and get threatened with being voted out of office when I suggest boosting revenue. Then you roll into town in your outrageous vehicle to complete a sentence that is just another publicity scheme for you. So, yes, I'm angry!"

His expression changed from frustration to devilment in an instant. "You're so sexy when you're mad," he said, pulling her the rest of the way across the desk and locking his mouth over hers.

She was so startled that she couldn't respond, couldn't think, for a moment. This was Wyatt, kissing her. She tried to push him away, but she was off balance and only managed to grab his shirt. She tried to protest, to tell him to stop, but the moment her lips parted he pushed his tongue into her mouth and deepened the kiss.

Her head swimming, she moaned and resisted, torn between breaking free and hauling him across the desk to have her way with him, right on top of her monthly planner.

"Um, Mr. McCall?"

Cassie's voice cut through the tension in the office, a strident sound in contrast to Toni's heavy breathing. Wyatt's hands tightened on Toni's arms and she couldn't move.

"We have an appointment with the reporter and photographer from the Graham newspaper. Er, at the community center. Now."

Breathing hard, Toni stared at Wyatt. He looked nearly as stunned as she felt. Finally, he released her arms and stepped back. She practically collapsed into her desk chair.

"I guess we'd better continue our conversation later," he said, pulling his flannel shirt closed and buttoning it low, near his waist. Only then did Toni realize he was concealing the effect of their sudden kiss from Cassie's eyes.

Toni felt her cheeks heat as her embarrassment grew. Wyatt had done it again! Made her revert to her teen years, seem silly and weak in front of someone else. She was sure Cassie believed that the kiss was mutual.

"There's nothing to talk about. Nothing of consequence, anyway."

"We'll see about that, babe."

"Don't call me that!"

He grinned, turned and strode out of the door. Cassie looked back for just a minute, appearing distressed, and mouthed, "Sorry." Then she hurried after Wyatt. Toni hoped Cassie would immediately erase the image of her boss kissing the mayor from her memory.

Toni sank back into her chair. For a moment, she had to admit, she had kissed him back. But only for a moment, and only because she was surprised.

And because this was Wyatt, the only person who ever made me crazy, she thought grudgingly.

Shaking her head to clear the feel and smell of him, the memories of the hundreds of kisses they'd shared, she sat up straight and braced her hands on her desk. She had to get back to work. She had things to accomplish today and every day.

If she kept herself busy enough, perhaps she wouldn't think of Wyatt much at all. Not more than once an hour, if she was lucky.

And she wouldn't see him again for hours. She'd get through the dinner party tomorrow night, and then maybe she wouldn't see him until it was time for him to leave town again. He could get his publicity photos for the local paper, which would no doubt be picked up by the national press, and he'd forget all about hiring a design firm to turn the community center lawn into a holiday extravaganza.

"THE SCOUTS HAVE DONE a wonderful thing for Brody's Crossing by adding these animated reindeer and bright trees to the community center grounds. I hope to expand on their generosity this year," Wyatt told the female reporter, who was probably a few years older than his thirty-three.

"What do you have in mind?"

He grinned and winked at her. "It's a surprise. Come back Saturday night and you'll see."

"We'll do that, Mr. McCall." She smiled and turned off the recorder, then looked up again. "If we could take a few photos of you by the display, that would be great. I think the light's about perfect now."

He posed with his hand on the reindeer, then stood with arms folded among the lighted spiral trees, and finally he hunkered down next to the colorful gift boxes. Thankfully, time and the cool temperature had simmered him down enough so that he could now unbutton his flannel shirt without showing the world that Miss Mayor had given him a flagpole of an erection.

Even before he'd kissed her, he'd become so aroused that all he wanted to do was drag her off—preferably someplace close and private—and make love to her until they were both sated. He wasn't sure how long that would take, since they'd been apart for fifteen years, but he was willing to give it a good try.

Considering her testy mood and his building impatience, he might even approach the task as a public service. Much more enjoyable than assembling Christmas lawn ornaments.

"Thank you, Mr. McCall," the photographer said, snapping Wyatt's attention back to the present.

"Sure, no problem," he replied with another grin. "You just call my public-relations director here if you need anything else." The reporter smiled, appeared a little rattled and waved as she and the photographer walked back to her white car with its magnetic sign on the side.

Wyatt sighed as he and Louisa stood in the late-afternoon gloom. Clouds had come in, which had allowed the lighted decorations to really show up for the photographs. Or at least, he hoped so. He didn't want to have to do this again until the final display was ready.

He heard the door to the Hummer slam and watched Cassie walk over, her phone and notepad clutched to her body.

"I found a designer who has decorations!" she said, almost glowing as she stopped beside them. "Someone ordered them to go in front of his business, but then he went broke and the designer was stuck with a large number of extra outdoor decorations. He's sending photos and a contract to my e-mail."

"That's great. When can he be here?"

"Right away, he said. Everyone else had their installations set up before Thanksgiving."

"Excellent. The parade is Saturday. I want the town to look spectacular by that night."

"That only gives him two days."

Wyatt looked at his watch. "Two and a half if he gets loaded right away." Despite what Toni thought, he was going to get this done *and* make sure the Scout troops were honored. This would be the best damn Christmas ever in Brody's Crossing, even if he had to spend a fortune and work his ass off to get it done.

Then he could leave knowing he'd accomplished what no one else had done for the town, and everyone would be happy.

Maybe not satisfied in every sense of the word, but happy. Glad that Wild Wyatt McCall had come to town and left it intact. No big incidents. Nothing embarrassing. Just some nice Christmas decorations and smiles all around.

Yep, that's what he was going to do.

Chapter Four

Toni looked out her front windows on Thursday morning to see a police car, two large panel trucks, a half-dozen pickups and at least a dozen people in front of the community center. Onlookers stood on the sidewalks, sipping their morning coffee and gazing at the activity. Off to the side, Wyatt conferred with Chief Montoya and community center director, Martha Chase. She was, as usual, animated and energetic about whatever they were discussing. As Toni watched, more citizens joined the onlookers. Soon they would have a sizable crowd lining Elm Street.

"This doesn't look good," Toni whispered as she let the curtain fall. She rushed to her bedroom and pulled on jeans and an old Dallas Stars sweatshirt, stuffed her feet into shoes and headed for the front door.

She completed a fast walk across the street in seconds, eavesdropping on the conversation as she went. Wyatt was up to something, that was for sure.

"This could be a safety issue," Chief Montoya was saying, pointing to tall poles that circled the wooded lawn of the center. Apparently they were erecting some type of fence.

"If you're worried, I'll provide security," Wyatt said.

"We want the surprise factor!" Martha insisted.

"What's going on?" Toni asked, slightly out of breath as she approached the group.

"Chief Montoya is being unreasonable," Martha said to Toni. "Mr. McCall has arranged for a truly spectacular Christmas display as a surprise to the town, but for some reason the police want to stop us."

"I'm not trying to stop the display. Just do it out in the open, where we can protect the citizens and also the decorations. If everything is concealed, we can't see if anyone breaks in to steal or damage the items, whatever they are."

"Then it won't be a surprise!" Martha said, throwing up her arms. She was obviously strongly on Wyatt's side. No shocker there. He could sweet-talk anyone, from toddler to grandmother, as long as the person was female.

"Are you building a fence?" Toni asked Wyatt.

"Yes, for privacy, just until the chili supper." The annual event, usually held the next weekend, was taking place on Saturday evening in honor of Wyatt's return to town. "I'd like for everyone to get their first glimpse as they arrive at the center. Besides, the unveiling should increase attendance and make more money for the food bank and clothing closet."

He had a point. The local charities raised much of their annual budget and received useful merchandise through the chili supper proceeds and donations. "Can you provide security?"

Wyatt shrugged. "Sure. I'm certain we can hire some off-duty police from Brody's Crossing or Graham, or even recruit some Young County deputies. Everyone needs extra cash at Christmastime, right?"

Another good point. "Chief, would that be acceptable to you?"

"As long as the area is patrolled. We can send cars by, but if the fence is opaque, as Mr. McCall has said, we can't see what's going on inside without doing a search. And also from what he's said, there will be some pretty big items there, which perps could hide behind."

"Oh, for heaven's sake, it's a Christmas display!" Martha

exclaimed. "Who in this town is going to try to harm it or steal it or whatever?"

Everyone except Martha turned to look at Wyatt. This type of situation was just the sort of thing that would have tempted him when he was around fourteen.

"Don't look at me. I'm all grown up and responsible now. Are there any young versions of me running around town these days?"

"No, thank God," Toni said.

Wyatt narrowed his eyes and frowned at her.

"An off-duty officer or even a rent-a-cop would be fine with me," Chief Montoya said. "We'll do drive-bys also."

"Okay, then. We need to get back to work," Wyatt stated. He waved at two men who were waiting by the panel trucks. "Go ahead with the fencing."

"I'm sure this will work out just fine," Toni told Martha. "We have to be careful of anything that will be on public display."

"I just want the citizens to have something spectacular— not that the reindeer and such aren't wonderful, too. Mr. McCall has promised a winter wonderland, and I can't wait to see the result." She hugged her arms over her heavy sweater. "Come in for some coffee or tea before you leave if you'd like," she told Wyatt, then turned and went back into the building.

"So," Toni said, folding her arms on her chest against the chill, and also because she was slightly miffed at Wyatt's secrecy. Especially after their conversation yesterday. And what happened while they were talking. "What do you have planned?"

"It's a secret," he said, smiling down at her. "You'll have to wait for the unveiling just like everyone else."

"I'm the mayor. I need to know what's going on."

"Winter wonderland, that's what," he said. "I'm not telling."

"That's so juvenile."

"It will be fun."

"I want to see what you have planned before the public unveiling."

"You don't trust me."

"You've got that right."

"I'm wounded," he said, and put his hand over his heart. "How can you think I'd do anything to harm the town?"

"Oh, let me count the ways. Streaking. Disrupting the Settlers' Stroll. Creating a public nuisance. Driving without a license. And let's not forget the one that got you into the most trouble, painting the water tower."

"Years ago. Water under the bridge," he said with a dismissive wave. "I'm older now. Besides, I'm trying to do something nice for the town, as I told you yesterday."

"I remember. Pardon me if I don't believe every word you say."

"You should have more faith in me."

"I don't trust you any farther than I could throw you."

"You want to get naked and wrestle?"

"Oh!" Toni felt her face blaze. Thankfully, the crowd was standing back and Wyatt had spoken rather softly, so they hadn't heard his entirely inappropriate comment. Toni turned on her heel and stalked back across the street.

Wyatt's laughter followed her all the way into the house. "Cretin," she growled under her breath. "I wouldn't look at his display if he were the last man on the earth."

She would avoid him all together, since the director and the police chief had already agreed to his ridiculous plan of keeping secrets. Fine. She would go on record with a memo, explaining her opposition to their plan. If he tried to pull anything…she didn't want to be responsible.

Wyatt McCall might just cause her to develop ulcers before he left town.

And thinking of ulcers reminded her that she might have indigestion fairly soon, as she had to attend his parents' dinner party tonight. Where she would no doubt have to watch him charm everyone into forgetting what a scoundrel he really was.

NOT EVEN FACING A BORING dinner party at his parents' house could dampen Wyatt's mood. The eight-foot, black, vinyl, mesh fence had gone up quickly on metal poles and the trucks had unloaded the most fantastic decorations he'd seen in years. The community center was going to look like a true fantasy wonderland. Wyatt had also supervised preparations for the new home of the reindeer and spiral trees. The Scouts would not be disappointed.

Even hiring off-duty cops hadn't been a problem. They were happy with the double-overtime wages they were receiving for patrolling the property. Since the display crew had filled up the remaining rooms at the Sweet Dreams Motel, this was a win-win situation for everyone in town.

Tonight, Louisa and Cassie were hosting an impromptu party for the workers and community center staff at Dewey's, and they'd all been warned to keep quiet about what was being installed. Cassie had even decided to try country-western dancing, and Louisa was taking photos to upload onto the Web page later.

Wyatt thought it odd that he had to have a Web page or a blog about his public life, but Louisa insisted it was a good idea to focus everyone on his philanthropic and charitable work. If it helped the foundation, he'd go along, but it still seemed silly to put any emphasis on *his* activities, especially when he was only doing what was right.

After making sure everything went well at the community center, he headed back to the motel with Cassie and Louisa, handing them the keys to the Hummer when they arrived. Everyone had to get ready for tonight. He needed to check his e-mail and authorize a transfer of funds to the foundation. And then he had to make a phone call.

After shutting down his laptop, he dressed in a black silk T-shirt, charcoal slacks instead of his usual jeans and a black leather jacket. That was as formal as his attire could get without making a shopping trip or arranging a special delivery from his wardrobe in Carmel. The weather was nice, and the forecast was favorable for the new Christmas display. High winds or rain could prove disastrous to their plans for that winter wonderland.

He settled back in the chair in his honeymoon suite, then dialed the number from the business card Toni had given him.

"Hey, babe—I mean, Miss Mayor. I need a favor."

"I CAN'T BELIEVE YOU have to bum a ride with me to your own parents' dinner party," Toni said as soon as Wyatt climbed into the seat of her extended-cab pickup. At least she didn't have a tiny little car, where he'd be right next to her. Of course, as he stretched out his left arm and his legs, he seemed to take up the whole front seat.

"Louisa and Cassie needed a vehicle tonight. They're going to take a group to Dewey's. I couldn't strand them with a bunch of workers they don't know."

Okay, that was probably true, but still… "It seems awfully convenient. Them taking a group to Dewey's on the same night that your parents are having a party in your honor."

"The workers are only going to be here a couple of days. Besides, it's just dinner at my parents' house," he said with a trace of defensiveness.

"They've never had a dinner for you before where city officials were invited." She glanced at Wyatt as she stopped at the traffic light on Main Street at Commerce. The McCalls had invited her to the house as part of the city council when they hosted an event. They treated her exactly as they would anyone else, as though she'd never been a big part of Wyatt's life.

He shrugged. "Maybe they just got the Christmas spirit."

"Maybe." But she doubted it. The McCalls weren't the most warm and fuzzy people she knew, although they were generous enough with their money. They did love the town and their only son, but they weren't overly social on a personal basis. Of course, Mrs. McCall especially had her reasons for being reserved and private. She'd never talked about her problems with anyone as far as Toni knew, but few secrets were really kept in a small town.

"You know," Wyatt said as he shifted position, "my mother thinks you're doing a great job as mayor."

"That's nice of her to say." Margaret and Bill McCall had never been wild about Toni when she was dating Wyatt. She hadn't known why, exactly. Perhaps Mrs. McCall had had bigger plans for her son. The Casales hadn't been wealthy with land and oil, but they'd always been business owners and had gotten by without experiencing the financial crises common to ranchers. For whatever reason, Toni had always felt a bit of chill from Wyatt's mother.

His mother shouldn't have worried; Wyatt had no intention of taking their relationship anywhere. Unlike some of their classmates who dated through high school, went off to college together or just got married right after graduation, Wyatt couldn't wait to get out of town and leave his teenage "sweetheart" behind.

Toni had felt as if their three years together had been wasted, nothing but a lie. She'd felt deceived and hurt, and when she was totally honest with herself she still blamed Wyatt for playing her like a fool.

She'd gotten over him, though, except when she was angry with him. Which was only when he came back to town, or when someone mentioned him or she saw a photo in a magazine. Not all the time, not anymore.

"You're quiet tonight," Wyatt said as Toni drove northwest out of town toward the ranch. The sun had already set, but some purple-and-orange streaks remained in the dark sky.

"I've got a lot on my mind. The renovations to the old hotel, the parade Saturday afternoon, the upcoming budget meetings and last but not least, your secret project at the community center. Oh, and to top everything off, I have to decide whether I'm running for office again. So, yes, I do have a lot to consider."

"Why wouldn't you run for office again?"

Of course he picked up on the one thing that she didn't really want to discuss. "Maybe it's time to concentrate all my energy on my business."

"You've been doing both for how long now?"

"Three years. Four, as of next election."

"You're the youngest mayor in Brody's Crossing history."

"Probably."

"Will you have an opponent in the primary or general election?"

"I don't know. I could."

"I think you should run again."

"Gee, thanks for the vote of confidence."

"What are you upset about?"

"Nothing." It's not as if she had anything better to do with her time. Like develop a personal relationship. Get married and have children. How could she do those things while in office? She barely had time for a minimal social life with family, much less try to find a man. Plus, the pool of bachelors in Brody's Crossing was shrinking fast, thanks to Christie Simmons Crawford, Raven York and Sandy Brody. Not that Toni had ever been interested in Cal, Troy or James.

"You are, too. I made you upset, and I didn't mean to. Not this time. So tell me what I said."

"We don't have to discuss this. Let's just say that maybe I have plans for my life that I can't pursue if I'm spending a big percentage of my nonprofessional life on city business."

"You mean, as in your personal life? Do you have a secret boyfriend?"

"No!" As if she could keep a relationship a secret.

"But you're thinking about it, right? Anyone I know?"

"No. I am not in a relationship or thinking about having one with anyone in particular."

"With the male population in general, then," he said. "You're looking, aren't you? Thinking about looking?"

"You make it sound so tawdry. No, I am not looking."

"Humph," he said, crossing his legs so that he took up even more room in the cab of her truck.

"Just don't start on me tonight, okay? I'm going to be nice to your parents and have dinner, then I'm going home and mark off one more day on my calendar until you're finished and out of here."

"That's cold, Toni. What have I done…lately, that is, to make you angry?"

She slowed, pulling into the long drive to his parents' house, and gave him a look as they rolled to a stop. "Yesterday afternoon," she said. "My office."

"Oh, yeah." She could see his flashing white teeth even in the dim light of the interior. "Well, no one but Cassie knows."

"What matters is that you did it."

"Go ahead and say it. It matters that I kissed you."

Toni thumped her head against the headrest, again and again. "What did I do to deserve you? Why am I being punished?"

Wyatt laughed. "If you don't move this truck, you're also going to get honked at."

Toni turned around and looked at headlights right on her rear bumper. "Great." She took her foot off the brake and headed toward the house. Hopefully, Wyatt had gotten all his foolishness out during the ride here. If she was lucky, he would leave her alone the rest of the night.

She was *not* taking him home. Back to the motel. Let him bum a ride with someone who liked to be around billionaire bad boys.

UNDER MOST CIRCUMSTANCES, Wyatt found dinner parties boring. Dinner with his parents and their friends had added potential to be a yawner. However, sitting next to Toni, who was obviously still miffed about that kiss in her office, gave the food some serious appeal.

His mother served a standing rib roast, complete with little white fancy "boots" for the rib bones. The beef was presented with roasted potatoes and some sautéed green beans with almonds. He watched Toni pick at her food, eating more potatoes than meat, and breaking a dinner roll into small pieces. He'd known her long enough to know she was about ready to jump out of her chair and drive off in that big pickup truck of hers.

Without him, of course.

"Dinner is delicious, of course," George Russell, president of the bank, said to Wyatt's mother. George was a big eater and loved a free meal almost as much as he loved a big depositor in his bank. "You always serve the best, Margaret."

Wyatt wanted to roll his eyes at the obvious sucking up. His parents had considered changing banks last year, shifting their business to a new branch in Graham. George Russell was still trying to get them to stay at First National with compliments rather than good service and competitive interest rates.

To distract himself from his parents' situation, beneath the level of the tabletop he broke off a bit of his roll and tossed it at Toni. The little piece landed on her folded hands. Her head jerked up, her eyes big and round.

He raised his eyebrows and shrugged. She frowned and seemed to turn her attention back to the table, but he knew she wasn't interested in hearing the other guests talk about a fishing trip to Minnesota. He took another piece of roll and tossed it at her arm, bare from just below the elbow down to her plain, sensibly manicured fingernails. The top she wore was a soft, dark blue velvet that draped at her neck and only hinted at what was beneath.

Wyatt remembered, though, and he wondered how much she'd changed in all these years. Was she still as sensitive?

The bread missed the mark, falling to the floor. Wyatt took another piece and aimed a bit higher. This time, he managed to land the crouton-size morsel on her chest, where it almost immediately disappeared under the drape of her velvet top.

She jumped and looked at him. He couldn't hide a smile at the thought of making that three-point shot into her cleavage.

"Excuse me, please," Toni said to his mother and the table in general. When she popped up from her seat, he did the same and pulled the chair back.

"What are you doing?" she whispered fiercely as she turned her head toward his.

"Being a gentleman," he whispered back.

"By pelting me with bread crumbs?"

He chuckled. Louder, he asked, "Do you know where the powder room is?"

"Yes, I believe I can find it. Alone." Toni hurried off.

He sat back down and sipped a little more of his wine. Someone had chosen a nice Napa Valley cabernet. Not his parents. They had no interest in wine. The two of them were drinking iced tea tonight.

Just before he expected Toni's return, he took his empty glass and excused himself to the kitchen. In the short hallway to the left, he intercepted her as she walked toward the dining room.

"Are you going to give me a ride home?"

"No, I hadn't planned on allowing myself such a pleasure."

"Ah, you're getting sarcastic. That's so sexy."

"No, it's not. Neither are bread crumbs in my... Never mind."

"Sorry about that. I was aiming at your arm."

"You shouldn't be aiming at me at all."

"I was bored. I was dreading a slide show of dead fish

shots. Or maybe a photo album of the fishing trip, including a recital of all the songs sung on the road."

That made Toni smile. Just a little, and he could tell she was trying not to be amused. "I have a busy day tomorrow. I'm going home in a few minutes, and I wouldn't think of having you cut your visit short."

"I don't mind."

"I'm sure James and Sandy Brody will give you a ride back to the motel."

"They're driving her new sports car. There's barely a backseat."

"Then the Russells. I know they have a Buick."

"Have you seen how thick his glasses are? I'd be scared to death to ride with him."

Toni laughed out loud, quickly putting her hand over her mouth. "You, who paraglide off cliffs and mountain bike in the Grand Canyon, would be afraid of a middle-aged banker?"

"I value my life. Riding in the backseat of the Russells' Buick is too scary to consider." He leaned a little closer. "Besides, if you give me a ride home, I promise I'll give you a preview of the Christmas decorations before we take the fence down for the big reveal."

"You will? I mean, you should—I am the mayor, after all."

"Of course. I was just kidding about it being a secret from you. I meant it was a secret for the town."

"That's not what you said."

"I was joking. How about tomorrow night? We'll light it up and I'll show you a special feature you won't believe."

"Tell me, Wyatt."

He tilted his head a little and smiled at her. "I think that's the first time you've said my name without cursing me."

"I don't curse you."

"Maybe you should."

She looked away. "No, I try not to curse anyone."

He touched a strand of hair that had fallen in front of her ear. "Even juvenile delinquents who go off and leave you?"

"That was a long time ago," she whispered.

"Sometimes it doesn't feel like all that long ago. Sometimes, when we're together, I feel like I'm eighteen again."

Toni stepped back, her expression blank. "Well, whenever you feel that way, just head back to California. I'm sure the sensation will go away quickly."

Chapter Five

Toni kept busy all day Friday, continuing with the demolition at the old hotel and working on the city budget during lunch and in the afternoon. She kept her mind occupied to keep from thinking about last night's dinner party, her bread crumb–throwing companion and their almost-intimate encounter near the kitchen. For just a moment there… But she wasn't going to think about how he'd whispered and nearly apologized for shaking up her life fifteen years ago.

Or maybe she'd imagined that he'd seemed sorry for his actions. Whatever his meaning or his feelings, she couldn't allow herself to be taken in by his charm. And there was no doubt about it—Wyatt McCall was a charmer.

She'd gotten out of giving him a lift back to the motel by pleading a pressing need to go back to her office in front of the other guests. James and Sandy Brody had given Wyatt a ride, thankfully, cramming him into the tiny backseat of their car. Toni was sure he'd be uncomfortable, but she didn't feel guilty.

She knew that she simply couldn't allow him to ride in her pickup again, especially at night when he was in such a mood, going from childish and irritating to mature and sexy in the blink of an eye.

Being with Wyatt while they were in high school had been like being on a ride at Six Flags, except that the end was never the same. The drop was different each time, the twists and turns unanticipated, the destination unknown. She'd both loved and dreaded his high-energy passionate nature.

They might never have survived that much turmoil. *She* might not have emotionally survived Wyatt's lifestyle. Sitting next to him at the dinner table, now that they were both adults, was nerve-racking enough to prove that they weren't meant to be together.

But tonight…tonight he was going to show her the community center Christmas display. She'd watched the workers unload supplies and enter the closed-off area this morning as she sipped her tea, and then she'd made a point of driving by several times during the day. They kept up a steady pace, despite the small crowd of people who stopped to watch them go in and out of the black vinyl-covered gate carrying huge cardboard boxes and items wrapped in packing material. A few people Toni saw during the day had asked her what Wyatt had planned, and all she could say was that it was a big secret.

He'd better not mess this up. Not at Christmas.

She worked until after six o'clock, and just when she thought he'd forgotten his promise, he called.

"Where are you?"

"At my office."

"Are you going home soon?"

"Probably. I was waiting to hear from you."

"I want you to walk over around ten o'clock, after the community center closes and the neighborhood has rolled up the sidewalks."

"That's kind of late."

"I'm not going to be ready until then. The installers are staying until nine, and then I'm going to finish up with a few final details."

"I do want and need to see the display, so if ten o'clock is the magical time, then that's when I'll be there."

"Is that even a word? I wasn't bossy."

"Oh, please. You were a born leader and you know it. People followed you right off the cliff."

"Not literally," he defended.

"Yes, they did. Remember that paraglider you bought?"

"Oh, well, that was just… No one broke anything."

"Only because you were as lucky as you were foolish."

"Stop with the compliments or I'll get a big head."

"Can we please call a truce long enough for me to see the Christmas decorations before I go back home? I have a busy day tomorrow."

"Ah, yes. The parade. Okay, then. Step forward and let me turn you just right." He adjusted Toni's body with as much touching, bumping and holding as he thought he could get away with.

"Wyatt!"

"Okay, open your eyes."

He removed his hands and stepped beside her to watch her expression.

"Oh. Wow." She took it all in. Five-foot-diameter shiny ornaments in gold, green, silver and red lay beneath the trees. The ornaments were lit from within, giving them a shimmering glow. Glistening red-and-blue ribbons rippled up to four feet high through the display and around the trees. Silver tinsel and even giant ornament hooks were scattered across the ground, which was covered in a blanket of artificial snow. More tiny lights were hidden beneath the ribbons and snow. The display was oversize, but proportional, as if waiting for a giant to come along and decorate a hundred-foot-tall tree.

"I've never seen anything like this. It's…it's magical."

"Yeah, I thought you'd like it."

"How did you… What is that snow?"

"It's an all-natural biodegradable product that will wash away once Christmas is over. Or sooner, if it rains, unfortunately. Let's pray for dry conditions and low winds through the month of December."

"Yes, let's," Toni said, walking forward. She kicked at the loose snow, sending it cascading as if it were real. "It's not cold."

"No, temperature is not an issue. Just water."

"This is so beautiful. How did you know what to get?" She strolled among the ornaments, her fingers lightly grazing the shiny globes.

"Honestly, I bought what was available. Cassie got on the phone and found this decorator who had been stood up by his client. This display was supposed to be in front of a retail store, but the owner couldn't pay due to financial trouble. I did the designer a favor by buying it all for the difference between the deposit and the full price he would have charged. And now we have a really spectacular Christmas display that will put everyone—including Graham—to shame."

"Christmas is not a competition," Toni said as she ran her hand along an undulating length of ribbon.

"No, but this will bring attention to the city. I'll bet people from around the area will drive here once they hear about it."

"You're spending a lot of money on the decorations, fence, installers and extra security."

Wyatt shrugged. "It's just money. It's not all that much, considering what I might be spending if I were back home or even traveling. Now, that's something that gets expensive."

"Because you go first-class?"

"Because I never know where I'll be going, and I'm impulsive and I decide to do things I probably shouldn't."

"Hmm, that's a good point." She looked up, the lights reflected on her face and hair. "Maybe we should have you come back every year to do this again."

He walked to where she stood and touched her hand as it rested on a gold ornament. "Maybe you should."

"Wyatt, don't—"

"Could we have that kind of relationship, babe? 'Same time, next year' always works in the movies."

"Movies aren't real life," she said, turning away. Walking away from him.

He wasn't ready to let her go. "Wait."

"Why?"

"I didn't tell you about the reindeer and the spiral trees."

"Oh. Yes, I should have asked," she said, shaking her head as if to clear her thoughts.

"We set up another area, facing the movie theater. I had a little hill built up. I think it's called a berm. That gave the white spiral trees a little more height and we could put the reindeer in what the designer called more 'natural' positions. As if white wire reindeer are natural," he said with a shrug.

"That sounds nice. And the presents?"

"Near the entry to the community center, one on either side of the doorway."

"Okay. Good." She shoved her hands into the pockets of her jacket. "I guess that covers everything, then. Thanks for the tour and I'll see you tomorrow at the parade, I suppose."

"Just a minute. There's something else you should see."

"What?" She sounded suspicious, as well she should be. He was making up excuses to keep her here longer.

"The peppermint candy. It's really pretty."

"I'm sure it is, but—"

He snagged her arm and pulled her through the ornaments to the other side of the display, which would be near the walkway when the fence was removed tomorrow.

"Wyatt, I appreciate the tour, but seriously—"

She tried to twist her arm away, so he took her hand in his and held on tight. "Just one more thing."

He heard a big sigh just before they rounded the last ornament, where a string of red-and-white peppermint candies lay nestled in the snow. The lights appeared even more muted and glowing.

"That is beautiful," Toni said softly.

"It's like being inside a dream or a fairy tale," Wyatt said. "I love this fantasy stuff."

"Maybe you missed your real calling. Perhaps you're a holiday designer at heart."

"Hmm. Maybe that will be my next profession." He stepped closer, still holding her hand. "Do you think there's much of a future for me designing holiday displays in Brody's Crossing? How about Easter and Fourth of July?"

"We don't decorate for Easter, but the Fourth of July has potential."

"Hmm. Good. I'll bet you look real good in red, white and blue."

"Wyatt, I don't think this is a good idea."

"You look good in anything. I've been fascinated by you ever since I walked into your office on Monday. You appeared different, yet the same. I wondered what you were wearing below the waist, because I couldn't see your legs. And then I saw them and you looked even better than you did when you were eighteen."

"Um, thanks, but really, you shouldn't—"

"Probably not," he said, pulling her closer. She wore a wary expression. "You still turn me on like crazy, babe. I can't stop thinking about you." He put his other arm around her waist and pulled her close.

"Wyatt, I can't…get involved."

"Then don't. Just kiss me now. No 'same time, next year.' No commitment and no promises."

"Just like before."

"No. Better. We're both adults. Just let me—let us—see what it would be like for just this moment."

"Oh, Wyatt," she whispered, her breath warm against the slight chill. "Everyone always said you could sell ice to Eskimos."

He smiled, dipped his head and kissed her slowly. Very slowly, savoring her soft lips and warm mouth, which tasted of hot chocolate. He pulled her tight, as close as they could get with several layers of clothes between them. Too many layers. He wanted to lay her down and remove every stitch. He wanted to see what the years had done to make her fuller, more toned, more mature. She had a woman's body that he wanted to explore more than he'd ever wanted to climb a mountain or sail an ocean. The teenage rush that he'd felt all those years ago came back full force. He felt as if he might explode, from his head to his toes. And especially in between.

Toni moaned and slid her hands beneath his leather jacket. Her short, round nails dug into his back. She tilted her head and sucked his tongue into her mouth, and his knees buckled.

They sank to the ground, cushioned by mounds of artificial snow. The peppermint candy garland snaked beside them, lighting them. Thank heavens for the light. At least he could see her face when they broke for air. He could locate her zipper and ease her jacket apart. Her breathing was as ragged as his as he braced himself above her, then lowered his weight and kissed her again. And again. Her legs twined with him and he felt as if he might well and truly explode from the raging desire. More than anything he'd felt in fifteen years. Maybe more than ever.

"Toni," he whispered, but didn't know what else to say. No promises, he reminded himself. They weren't meant to be together forever, but maybe they were meant for each other now.

He slid his hand beneath her soft T-shirt and cupped her breasts. She reached down and grabbed his butt, pulling him tight between her legs. "Yes," he whispered, and reached for the snap on his jeans.

"Mr. McCall! Mr. McCall, are you in here?" Across the

fenced-in area, the sound of a closing gate penetrated his consciousness.

"Wha… Who's that?" Toni asked, pushing him away.

"Night watchman," Wyatt whispered.

"No!"

"Unfortunately, yes," he said, easing her T-shirt down.

"Oh, God. How do I get myself into these situations with you?" She looked around. The snow was all messed up and some of the wires to the hidden lights were exposed.

"I told you we couldn't make snow angels in this stuff," Wyatt said in a loud voice. "Tom, we're over here. Everything's fine.

"Make a snow angel," Wyatt whispered to Toni as he rolled away. She looked stunned, but finally started moving her arms and legs. Not as he'd hoped, but she did make a passable attempt at angel wings.

The beam of light from a bobbing flashlight danced off the more subtle lights of the ornaments and ribbons. "You sure, Mr. McCall? That gate was closed, but it wasn't locked."

Wyatt sat up from his own snow angel, which was quite a mess. "I was just showing our mayor around the display and she was so taken with the artificial snow, she just had to try to make a snow angel. Sorry I forgot to lock the gate."

"Oh, that's okay," Tom said, standing above them on the other side of the peppermint candy garland. "I just wanted to make sure no kids had gotten in here and done some foolishness. You can't trust those kids. Or those drunk adults. They get liquored up and look for trouble."

"No, you can't." Wyatt had to admit that this was just the type of forbidden fruit he'd been drawn to as a kid. Hell, he was an adult and he was doing something wrong here. And he'd paid for the display and the night watchman who'd caught him!

"We'll be leaving in a few minutes. I'll lock up this time for sure," he told the other man.

"Good night, then. 'Night, Miss Mayor," he said, tipping his hat at Toni, who was still sprawled on the ground.

"Er, good night," she said to the watchman.

Wyatt watched as the beam of light bobbed away, through the ornaments. "I don't suppose you want to make some more snow angels together, do you?"

"No!" She pushed herself up and began brushing herself off. "I can't believe I got caught kissing you again. By someone else," she whispered fiercely. "Why can't I keep my head around you? This is ridiculous."

"Unusual, but hardly ridiculous. After all, we're two healthy adults, we have memories, a history. It's very logical that we'd be drawn to each other."

"No, it's not. I...I can't like you."

"Why not? I like you. I've even forgiven you for telling that reporter that I skipped town."

"Gee, thanks. That was unintentional."

"So was this. What's the difference?"

"Embarrassment, for one thing. I nearly got caught in a very compromising position."

"Oh? And you don't think the world reading that I was an irresponsible teenager who blithely went off without completing my sentence in my hometown wasn't embarrassing? And might even compromise my kids-at-risk foundation?"

Toni sighed and her hand stilled. "Put that way, I can see your point. But still... What we were doing was about...you know. It's hardly the same as painting a water tower or decorating a community center lawn."

"No, it's not the same. But, babe, that doesn't mean it wasn't real." He dusted himself off. "Come on, I'll lock up and walk you home."

"It's just across the street."

"Then I'll watch to make sure you get inside okay."

"I'm safe in Brody's Crossing." She zipped up her jacket.

"The only person I'm not safe from is you." She stalked off, winding her way through the ornaments.

"You've got that right," he whispered as he followed her out of the maze.

Chapter Six

The annual Brody's Crossing Christmas Parade was not to be missed. Anyone who wasn't in the parade watched along the streets as the flatbed trailer floats, marching bands, antique cars, mounted sheriff's posse, Scout troops and other groups wound through the downtown. The parade assembled in the high-school parking lot and made its way down Main Street, turned on Commerce, continued on Elm and made a square back to Main on Newcastle Drive. There were plenty of places to watch, applaud and accept favors and candy from the participants.

The highlight each year was the holiday princess float, on which various young ladies from thirteen to eighteen smiled and waved, their hair styled to perfection and their gowns identical. Toni's best friend had been a holiday princess, but Toni had never been interested in that distinction. She would much rather have watched or worked on the float itself, instead of being primped to within an inch of her life.

Today there was much joy in the air. The newly renovated businesses brought fresh spirit to the town, and there was a real buzz about Wyatt's surprise at the community center later today. Some of the outlying farm and ranch families were staying in town after the parade, waiting for the unveiling and the chili supper. There were even a few members of the press and photographers, probably in town to cover Wyatt.

Toni stood there in the mild weather on this sunny Saturday afternoon and did her best not to think about the yet-to-be-revealed Christmas decorations. The amazingly soft blanket of white. The snow angels that might still be visible between the ornaments and peppermint candy garland. She hoped that Wyatt had gone back and eliminated any trace of her visit to the area.

She'd reported to her fellow city council members that the display was all-age appropriate, spectacular in scope and appeared safe. That's all they were interested in, anyway.

They didn't want to know that their mayor had nearly done the wild thing in the middle of the community center lawn.

She would have moaned and put her head between her hands for the tenth or eleventh time today except that she had to get ready to depart the high-school parking lot on the back of a restored 1964 Pontiac LeMans convertible. Last year, she'd ridden on a locally owned vintage Thunderbird, but Christie had reserved that car early because she'd used it for the Fourth of July parade last year, during which Cal Crawford had proposed as she'd sat on the fender. Christie had a special affinity for the Thunderbird, which she used to promote the Sweet Dreams Motel on every available occasion.

"Okay, time to move out," city secretary Eileen Breslin said. She strode with purpose among the lined-up vehicles, her clipboard in hand. "Remember to keep an even distance from the vehicle or group in front of you. If you have any problems, pull out of the parade and wait for assistance. Now, let's have fun out there!"

Toni's driver helped her perch on the back of the seat. She pulled down the tight sleeves of her red velvet dress and spread the flared skirt around her, covering her legs all the way to her tall black boots. The dress was rather plain, but it gave a holiday impression with its scoop neck and fitted bodice. She wore a ruby-and-diamond heart pendant that her parents had given her for college graduation and small dangling ruby earrings she'd bought for herself when she was elected three years ago.

She was as ready as ever, yet she felt as if everyone would know what she'd almost done last night. Guilt was a feeling that she didn't experience on a regular basis. She wasn't secretive or manipulative, preferring to keep her business and her politics as aboveboard as possible. Until Wyatt had come to town, that is. Now she had guilty secrets, and she didn't like it one bit.

She wasn't in the habit of letting others know about her personal life, but now she couldn't even discuss her near indiscretion with her friends or family. She was expected to adhere to higher standards than, say, an eighteen-year-old on spring break.

This was all his fault.

"Is something wrong?" Eileen asked, standing next to the car.

"No." Toni sat up a little straighter. "Why?"

"You were frowning. You never frown."

"Sorry. Um, this dress is a little uncomfortable." She hated lying to Eileen. Another black mark against Wyatt.

"No wonder. Looks like you were sewn into it. It looks good, though. You're the sexiest mayor ever, and I can say that because I'm older than you are by a bunch and I've got three kids."

"Eileen! I was going for holiday appeal. Happy, red, velvet. Kind of elegant."

"You got naughty Mrs. Santa instead."

Toni covered her face with her hands. "Oh, no."

"Hey, I'm just kidding. Sort of. You look great. The crowd will love you."

"Not too much, I hope."

Eileen laughed. "It's too early in the day for rowdy cowboys. You should be safe."

"Gee, thanks for the words of encouragement."

"No problem. Now you'd better get going. The float two in front of you just pulled out."

Toni settled back in position again, wishing she had a big red cape and a Santa hat to change her outfit into something respectable. Too late. She was in this parade for better or for worse. And with Wyatt McCall in town, she was betting on *worse*.

WYATT CAREFULLY CONSIDERED running up to the Pontiac convertible, grabbing Toni off the backseat and taking her someplace private. Very private. For a very long time.

What was she thinking, wearing that body-hugging stretch-velvet dress? And where had she gotten it? There was no Victoria's Secret store around here. If Santa's elves looked like Toni, there would be no Christmas deliveries. Santa would never leave the North Pole.

However, kidnapping Toni in the middle of the annual parade probably wasn't a good idea. For one thing, everyone would see him. He'd ruin Toni's reputation and her chances for reelection, and he might even tarnish his image as a *reformed* juvenile delinquent.

Still, getting her alone in that dress might be worth any price.

"The parade was especially nice this year," his mother said from her folding chair on Main Street. "All the new businesses make the holidays so much more festive, don't you think?"

"Yes, ma'am."

"And the stores are decorated so nice."

"Wait until you see the community center."

"I hope that's not too late. I don't like to be out after dark, you know."

"We're taking the fence down at four o'clock, about an hour after the parade."

"I'm sure you've done a wonderful job," his mother said, patting his hand. "You always were more talented than the rest of the young people."

"I got lucky with the decorations. I didn't design or make them myself, Mom."

"You were the one who thought of them, though."

Wyatt forced a smile and tried not to argue with his mother. She'd always thought he could do no wrong, even when he was as guilty as hell. Invariably, she wanted to think that someone else had gotten him into trouble, or had accused him because they were jealous or some other nonsense.

Sometimes he suspected that he did some of these things just to see if she would finally admit that he was at fault.

"I think I'd like to rest between the parade and seeing your decorations at the community center."

"You can rest at the motel. My room is real comfortable."

"Oh, I don't know. Are you sure the place is…decent?"

"Yes, Mom, I'm sure."

"It didn't used to be," she said with a sniff as she turned up her nose at the idea of the Sweet Dreams Motel pre-Christie Simmons Crawford's restoration.

"There's talk of the motel getting landmark status."

"Really? Well, wouldn't that be special for the town?"

"I think so." Brody's Crossing didn't have any historical markers or landmark buildings…yet. If Toni could get this approved by the state commission, it would be a feather in her cap as mayor.

"She's a good mayor. I always liked Antonia."

That wasn't exactly the way Wyatt remembered his mother's view on his girlfriend. "Don't get that girl pregnant" had been her strongest admonishment. "She'll bleed us dry and you'll be stuck here forever" had been the follow-up prediction.

Now, she seemed to be pushing him toward "Antonia" and she had even commented that he could move back to Texas since he didn't have to be in an office every day. His mother, the matchmaker? He wouldn't have believed it a week ago.

Wyatt didn't have much interest in the parade once the mayor's car passed by. After telling his mother that he'd find her when the parade ended, he wandered down Commerce

Street toward the railroad tracks. The trains had quit coming through Brody's Crossing a long time ago, and the majority of the buildings that were still vacant faced the old tracks.

Most people were watching the parade on Main Street, but he saw a few stragglers. He didn't know all their names, but they smiled and said hello to him. Told him that they were glad he'd come back, and were looking forward to seeing the community center. These were people who didn't know him well and therefore didn't feel the need to tell him to behave.

He stopped in front of the hotel where he'd seen Toni working with her crew and partners on Wednesday. They'd made good progress, if the full container of debris was any indication. He walked up the wooden ramp that covered the concrete steps and peered through the dirty windows. The interior gutted, the old place looked ready for a face-lift. This was a big project. He was glad Toni was doing well in her business. The fact that she was a woman hadn't seemed to hurt her in the construction industry. He'd heard nothing but good things about her.

Old friends, neighbors and classmates all wanted to tell him their views of his former girlfriend, once they realized he wasn't upset or offended by their remarks. He always smiled and took it all in, then said something like "that's great" and changed the subject. He didn't want them to start asking personal questions. Like how he felt about seeing her again. Whether there was any chance that he and Toni might get back together. Whether he was surprised she had never gotten married.

Why hadn't she gotten married? Was it really because she'd been too busy or was something else holding her back?

Like him.

Had he really messed with her mind when he left for college? They'd never talked about the future except in vague terms. He'd always steered the conversation away from talk of weddings or houses or even what they'd be doing in ten years. He hadn't promised her anything, and she'd never asked. Which was just the way he'd wanted it.

Wasn't it?

He shook his head and turned away from the hotel windows. All this nostalgia was making him think crazy thoughts. Coming back home for the week had been easy in some ways, but difficult in others. The easy part was remembering the traditions and the people he knew casually. The hard part was realizing he missed his friends, the places he'd known growing up and, most of all, Toni.

He'd get through the next few days. He'd promised his mother and father that he'd stay through tomorrow and go to church with them. Although he didn't have any pressing need to get back to California, he should probably fly back on Monday. Brian was handling things well and the foundation had a good director and staff. Wyatt realized he was more of a figurehead than an administrator, but he should still be involved.

Besides, he might get a sudden urge to go surfing in Australia or skydiving in Montana. He'd been thinking of hiking in Peru to see the newly opened ruins. If it wasn't the rainy season there, he might try that.

The problem was, wherever he went, he was going to miss the verbal sparring with Toni. He liked her spunk and the way she tried to resist him before melting in his arms like ice cream in August. She didn't *want* to want him, but she did, and damn it, he wanted her, too.

Could he honestly leave Brody's Crossing without going for that wild adventure?

Probably not, he told himself as he walked back to where his mother sat on the parade route. He wondered if he would be Toni's downfall, or if she would be his.

AS SOON AS THE PARADE concluded, Toni rushed to her office to take care of a crisis with one of her best employees, Oscar, who supervised hanging drywall. He'd called during the parade. His son had fallen out of their hayloft this morning and broken his arm. To make matters worse, Oscar's wife was away in Arizona until Tuesday with her sick mother. He was going to need an advance on his paycheck and Monday off to take the boy to the orthopedic doctor in Fort Worth.

She sat at her desk and wrote out a check, noting his account number on the back, then put it in an envelope. She'd volunteered to take it to the bank for him, since he was home with his son.

Maybe having children wasn't all it was cracked up to be. How would she manage to run her business, much less her job as mayor, if she had children she was responsible for? She had such tight deadlines on her jobs that she couldn't just take off if someone else needed her.

Fortunately, her mother and father were healthy and Leo lived in town again, so as a family they could depend on each other. She couldn't imagine what she'd feel like if she alone was responsible for a child or ailing parents. Maybe she was just selfish, thinking of her business and career while other women raised families and took time for parents and friends. Her high-school best friend, Jennifer, had a daughter who'd already gone through chemo and thankfully had survived. Of course, since Jennifer was married with a family, she and Toni didn't have much in common anymore, so they weren't close friends.

Friends. Now, that was another sore spot. Sometimes she wished she could be like those women on television, who had lots of girlfriends they could talk to about anything.

What would it feel like to say to Christie Crawford, "Do you think I was crazy when I was making out with Wyatt on the ground at the Christmas display the other night and we almost got caught by the night watchman?" The man could have been an off-duty cop from Brody's Crossing, for heaven's sake!

She was pretty sure Christie would agree that Toni was, indeed, crazy. On the off chance she said something like, "No, of course you're not crazy. Go for it!" then Toni wasn't sure what she'd do or say.

Talking to friends about men—about Wyatt—would be so complicated. Maybe she was better off keeping her "dear diary" thoughts to herself.

She shook herself out of her doldrums and put her checkbook away. She wrote a quick note to the bank teller explaining the deposit. After grabbing her purse and keys, she locked her office and made her way to the night depository. The crowds had dispersed after the parade, the barriers were off the streets and things were returning to normal. Some of the shops had reopened for business, but most remained closed so everyone could enjoy the afternoon.

The day was sunny, the air crisp as she walked briskly toward the bank next door. The night deposit was right next to the ATM machine, around the corner. After she took care of this errand, she was going straight home to change her clothes. Jeans and a sweater would be more appropriate for the chili supper at the community center. Then she wouldn't have to worry about anyone thinking naughty thoughts about her dress.

As if on cue, a loud wolf whistle split the blessed silence.

She turned in the direction of the offending noise and found her nemesis leaning against his parked Hummer on Main Street. Drawing a deep breath, she allowed herself a moment to take him in. Long legs in faded jeans, a leather jacket and an off-white waffle-weave sweater that showed off his tan. As he removed his sunglasses, his blue eyes sparkled and the sun streaks in his hair glistened.

They were the only people around for the moment.

"Are you whistling at yourself or at me?" she asked.

He grinned. "You, of course. That's some dress."

She held out the skirt and turned up her chin. "I think it's quite elegant."

"It's sexy as hell. That's what it is."

She dropped the velvet fabric and frowned. "I don't have time for this. We have to get ready for the unveiling."

"So? You have a little time. Come for a ride with me."

"Absolutely not! I need to change clothes."

"Why would you want to change out of that dress?" he asked, pushing away from the Hummer. "You look like the best Christmas treat ever." He walked toward her and she resisted the urge to step back. "A little whipped cream and some chocolate sauce would make you the perfect afternoon snack."

She gasped. Wyatt had never talked to her like *that*. She wanted to turn around and start running as fast as she could.

Not fast enough to outrun him, especially while she was wearing these high-heeled boots.

She waved the envelope at him. "I'm making this deposit and then I'm leaving. Alone. To change clothes."

"I'll give you a ride home."

"Oh, no. I don't trust you." How many times had he promised to drive her "straight home" and then detoured to make out—or more—before taking her back to her parents just in time for curfew? She'd lived in constant fear that they'd get caught, that they'd be late getting home, that something would happen and she'd disappoint everyone around her. The emotional highs and lows had been so intense…

She was older now, and wiser. She couldn't go back to those roller-coaster feelings.

"Come on, Toni. Don't make me chase you," he said with a grin.

"Don't you dare."

"Mr. McCall!" Cassie's voice once again cut through the tension, but this time Toni was grateful. Very grateful. She watched Wyatt's assistant almost jog toward them from the direction of the community center.

"The designer needs you at the display," Cassie said breathlessly. "A section of the lights won't come on, and the installers have already left."

Wyatt looked at Toni and smiled. "Looks like we won't be going for a ride, babe."

"We were not going for a ride!"

He grinned and turned away, his long strides eating up the distance to the Hummer. "I'll see you at the community center."

"And don't call me babe," she yelled after him.

Chapter Seven

A loose connection that just happened to be in the area where Wyatt and Toni had nearly made love had caused the lights to go out in one section. Disregarding the confusion of the designer over how the wires had become disconnected, Wyatt helped reconnect the strands. When he finished, one of Martha's employees flipped the switch and the lights came on.

He straightened as he heard the *oohs* and *ahhs* of the small group of people gathered on the sidewalk. They clapped their hands and Wyatt took a bow. He raised the hand of the designer, then encouraged the other man to take a bow also. When they finished their impromptu curtain calls, Wyatt grinned, dusted the fake snow off his jeans and walked into the community center.

He knew the basic expectations of the city officials, Martha and her employees. He would be introduced by Miss Mayor on the lawn of the center. She'd say nice things about him, then he would make some suitable remarks, and finally the people of Brody's Crossing would be invited to walk around the display. Martha would then invite them inside for chili.

This was just the kind of event that he would have been tempted to disrupt when he was a teenager. But tonight he would be on his best behavior. After all, the big unveiling was his last obligation to Brody's Crossing.

He'd wiped the slate clean, so to speak. So why didn't he feel relieved? Where was his sense of accomplishment? After all, he'd achieved his goal of providing a fantastic Christmas display. He'd done something nice for his hometown. He'd shown everyone that he could behave himself.

Well, almost everyone. He'd slipped a little on the good-behavior standard with Toni.

While he pondered when Toni might arrive from her house across the street and whether she'd still be wearing that killer dress, his mother and father arrived after having their rest at the motel. He greeted them, and they sat down with George Russell and several of their friends on some of the few chairs placed outside for "dignitaries." Standing nearby was the reporter from Graham, plus a few photographers.

Wyatt overheard his mother exclaim what a wonderful job he had done, as if he'd created the decorations personally. He wandered off to chat with some people he knew.

At five o'clock, as the sun began to set, he walked over to Martha Chase and a few others. Where was Toni? Then he saw her, striding up the walkway, smiling and greeting the folks gathered for the festivities. She was a born politician, always available and diplomatic.

"Miss Mayor," he said with a grin as she stopped before him. Regretfully—not that she didn't look good in anything—she'd changed into a red sweater and black jeans. He'd give about a year of his life to see her in that red dress again. And even more than that to take it off her.

"Are you ready for me to tell everyone how lucky we are that you're one of Brody's Crossing's favorite sons?" she asked as she stopped directly in front of him.

"There's that sarcasm again." He leaned forward and said softly, "I told you it turns me on."

"You claim that almost everything turns you on," she whispered fiercely. "I'm beginning to think you have serious issues. Maybe you should get a new girlfriend. I think you must be deprived."

"Oh, I'm deprived all right. Are you volunteering to ease my frustration level?" he countered softly, leaning toward her until they were almost nose to nose.

"You know darn well I'm not. Stop making those comments!"

"You brought it up."

"Um, excuse me," Martha Chase said, interrupting their private moment, held right out in the open. "Are we ready to begin?"

Toni blinked, straightened and seemed to shake herself free of their verbal sparring. "Of course, Martha. Is the microphone hooked up?"

"Yes. Just come this way, both of you."

"After you," Wyatt said. Walking behind Toni gave him an excellent view of those bottom-hugging jeans and black boots. The high heels made her tall enough to kiss without bending over—if he could just get close enough to convince her to kiss him again.

Only when they were standing before the podium did Wyatt realize that Christmas music was playing over the outdoor speakers. Nice touch. The music swelled, then went silent, as Toni called for everyone's attention.

"Thank you for coming today to the parade and also to the presentation of the new holiday decorations, generously donated by one of Brody's Crossing's most famous former residents, Wyatt McCall."

A round of applause interrupted Toni's speech, and Wyatt felt unexpectedly touched to hear the citizens of his hometown cheer for him. Or what he'd done for them.

"As you probably know, Mr. McCall now lives in California. He recently took his software company public and is now devoting time to a foundation for at-risk teens." Toni turned and gave him a look. Sort of a schoolteacher look. "Teens who get into trouble or have behavior issues, something that Mr. McCall has some familiarity with."

People chuckled, then applauded. Wyatt even felt his cheeks heat a little. He hadn't expected Toni to call him out. She must be really miffed with him.

"So, it is now my great pleasure to present Mr. McCall with this key to the city, which I'm sure he will cherish as he continues his good works back in California."

Wyatt stepped to the podium and accepted the giant silver key in its flat black velvet case. He tilted the case toward the audience, held it high and smiled. Flashes temporarily blinded him. Both the press and the townspeople took photos. He was now officially absolved of being a juvenile delinquent—or at least a former juvie with an unfinished civil sentence.

And as Toni had mentioned, he was free to go back to his life in California. As a matter of fact, she'd practically kicked him out of town. She must really want to get rid of him to mention that in her public comments.

"Thank you very much, Mayor Casale, and everyone in the municipal government. It has been great being back in Brody's Crossing." Applause interrupted him, then he continued. "I would also like to thank Martha Chase and her staff for their cooperation and support here at the community center." More applause. "Now, I'm not a believer in long speeches. Those of you who remember me know that I never liked to sit still for too long." Chuckles from everyone but his mother, who frowned from her seat on the front row.

"So, enjoy the decorations. Please take time to look at the new locations of the Scout troops' reindeer and trees, standing on their new hill where they can look over the lawn. And I know you'll appreciate the chili dinner. As a special incentive to encourage you to be generous with your donations to the food bank and other charities supported by tonight's event, I want to say that I'll personally match the amount of money donated tonight."

A big round of applause showed the town's appreciation of his impromptu remarks, so he smiled, held the key up once more and then stepped back from the podium. Martha Chase stepped forward, giving directions in her usual efficient style, and soon everyone was milling around the lawn, looking at the decorations.

Wyatt made a retreat to the community center. His role as benefactor was over.

After going through the line for his bowl of chili, Wyatt sat with Cassie and Louisa, James and Sandy Brody, the Maxwells, Cal and Christie Crawford and their little boy. The noise level in the community center was matched only by the smell of the chili simmering in big pots in the adjacent kitchen. Tables were covered with empty and partially full plastic bowls, baskets of crackers and corn bread, and bottles of hot sauce. Children ran around the tables and old friends filled the aisles, talking as if they hadn't seen each other in ages.

The aromas and sights were so familiar, yet so strangely foreign. Wyatt knew he'd done this many times during the first eighteen years of his life, yet he hadn't been to a community-type dinner in the past fifteen years. When he was a teenager, most of his time had been spent either trying to get into trouble or trying to get a girl to go outside with him. Now, there was only one girl he wanted, and that would definitely get them both into trouble.

Even so, he'd discovered he couldn't really help himself when she was around. Right now she was across the room with her parents and Leo, chatting and dipping her spoon into her chili, but barely eating.

"Do you want me to schedule our flight back to California for Sunday night or Monday?" Cassie asked.

"Hmm?" He wasn't ready to leave. "Weren't we going horseback riding? I still haven't arranged that."

"That's okay, Mr. McCall. I don't really—"

"No, I said I would, and since the weather is nice, we really should go." He turned to Louisa. "Why don't you see if any of the other media people want photos or interviews while we're here? Also, let's see if our designer has anything to replace those really lame silver tinsel decorations along Main Street. Those things are practically as old as I am."

Louisa made a note of both things. "I'll check with him before he leaves."

The designer had been invited to stay for the chili supper and had gotten quite a few congratulations from the citizens, both after the lighting and during supper.

"I suppose he's spending another night at the motel. Surely he won't drive back in the dark."

"He's staying," Christie said. "The motel manager mentioned it." She smiled at Wyatt. "This project of yours has really helped the local economy, especially at the motel. We've been booked solid all week."

"I told everyone we needed that motel," Ida Bell said.

"Toni did a great job," Christie said.

"She always does a great job," Burl Maxwell added.

"Is she going to run for reelection next year?" Wyatt asked.

"Oh, I think so. Why wouldn't she?" Ida said.

"I'm sure she will. She's a great mayor," Christie said.

"I agree," Wyatt said with a shrug, "but maybe she has other plans."

"Like what? Higher office?" Burl asked.

"I was thinking more along the lines of her career. Or maybe even her personal life."

"Oh, I don't know. She seems to handle everything so well," Ida said.

"Yes, she does," Wyatt agreed. She seemed to, at least. He wondered, though. Was she as happy as she seemed?

TONI TRIED TO SLIP OUT of the chili supper while Wyatt talked to old friends, but darn it, he must have seen her from the corner of his eye. He had the senses of a hawk…and she felt a lot like a scared rabbit. She walked faster toward her house, dodging the Christmas display. The ornaments, ribbons and snow had been spread out a little after the fencing had come down, so the display covered more space. The white faux flakes cushioned her steps as she cut across the lawn.

Her breathing increased as she walked faster and hugged her arms around her. She should have worn a jacket. The wind was cold despite the mild temperatures.

She jogged across her street and was almost to her small front porch when a man's low voice asked, "Are you going to invite me inside?"

She spun around, almost losing her balance in her high-heeled boots.

"Whoa! Be careful," he said, reaching out and steadying her with his hands on her arms.

His big, warm hands.

"I'm fine, thank you. I wouldn't have… Oh, never mind!" There was no sense telling him that he'd snuck up and startled her, despite the porch light she'd left on.

"This is a cute house," he remarked, looking up at her pitched roof, the dormer windows and shutters. She'd replaced much of the trim and restored the wooden siding when she'd bought the house four years ago. She had more plans for the cottage, which was so conveniently located that she could easily walk to her office or the city hall.

"I like it."

"I'd love to see the inside."

I'll just bet you would. "Maybe some other time. It's been a long day."

"My days are numbered, you know," he reminded her.

She hugged her arms around herself again. "I know. When are you leaving?"

"I haven't decided yet. I suppose I need some type of official approval."

"I guess so. That shouldn't be difficult. The display is great." She looked across the street. All the ornaments and lights seemed to be working properly. "You and the designer didn't have any trouble finding the problem earlier?"

"No. He wasn't sure what had caused it, but there seemed to be a place where some 'thrashing around' had gone on. He thought it was caused by a big raccoon." Wyatt leaned closer and said in a lower voice, "But you and I know better."

Despite the cold wind, Toni felt her cheeks warm. "Oh, for heaven's sake. Surely that wasn't the reason—"

"Yes, it was. But don't worry. I fixed it and I didn't say a thing. To anyone."

She heard the teasing in his voice, as if he'd like to hold such an indiscretion over her head. Or maybe she was just being paranoid. This wouldn't be the first time Wyatt had messed with her mind.

"You can come by the office Monday on your way out of town. We can even have an official photograph, if you'd like. I know Louisa uses that sort of thing for your publicity."

"For my foundation's publicity," Wyatt reminded her, no longer teasing. "I don't need publicity."

"Right."

"What? You think I want some photographer with a telephoto lens following me around, invading my life? It's a relief to get to a remote part of the world, whether I'm going to climb a mountain or surf a wave. There's no one there who cares if I have any money. Hell, most of the time there is no one there!"

"I'm not going to feel sorry for you because you made a fortune and travel around the world."

"I didn't ask for any sympathy. I was just correcting an apparent misconception you have about me and publicity."

"Consider me corrected." She stood on her porch and shivered. Wyatt looked so serious, so tense. He seemed to be waiting for her to make an offer. Come inside for coffee, wine or beer? She couldn't, though. She'd be inviting disaster.

"Just one more thing," he said after what seemed an eternity. "This town… I don't know if you realize it, but this week, people treat me just like they always did, except they've acknowledged that I'm older. Maybe not wiser, but no longer a teenager. I can be myself without running off to a remote mountain or deserted beach or isolated rain forest. It's good. It's something I didn't realize I missed."

"I hadn't thought about it, but I can see where that would be refreshing."

"I just wanted to tell you that. I know you think I'm still a kid at heart."

"I never said that."

"I can see it in the way you react to me."

She shifted her weight and frowned. "You keep me off balance, Wyatt. Just like you did when we were kids. I don't know what's coming next, except that I know it might get me in trouble if I'm not careful."

"Maybe you need a little trouble in your life."

"What does that mean?"

He shrugged. "You have everything so planned. So… orderly. You've done more than a lot of people do by the time they're fifty or sixty. I'm looking for evidence that you're enjoying your life, though."

"I am. I do."

"If you say so."

"What difference does it make to you? Before Monday, we hadn't talked in fifteen years."

He shrugged again. "Maybe I realized that's too long."

She threw up her hands. "You're doing it again! I have no idea how to take anything you say that's halfway serious."

"You shouldn't think about it so much. Life isn't always about logic, Toni. Sometimes, you just have to go with what feels right."

"Oh, no. That sounds like Wild Wyatt McCall logic, and that always got me into trouble."

He grinned. "I'll be in touch." He stepped back, still watching her.

"Wait! When are you leaving town?"

"I haven't decided yet."

"But the community center decorations are finished."

"I know, but I promised Cassie I'd take her horseback riding, and now I realize that we really should do something about those decorations along Main Street."

"The tinsel candy canes?"

"That's right. Even the description is horrible."

"Wyatt, you don't need—"

"I'll be in touch," he said again and turned, striding quickly down her short front walk. While she stood there and watched, he shoved his hands in his pockets and continued across the street to the community center. People were coming out, strolling by and looking at the decorations. Wyatt stopped to talk to someone, and Toni opened her front door.

She flipped on the foyer light and frowned. Wyatt had done it again. He'd confused her. He'd set her off on a roller-coaster ride of another type. His quiet confession that returning to Brody's Crossing was important to him, as important as his adventures abroad, gave her too much insight into Wyatt McCall, the man.

She'd known Wyatt, the boy. The man was much more dangerous.

ON SUNDAY, WYATT SAT THROUGH church with his parents, then begged off Sunday dinner by telling them that he was taking Cassie and Louisa horseback riding at the Brodys' ranch. He had to get back to the motel, change clothes and grab a bite to eat with his employees on the way to the ranch. Hopefully, they had some jeans and decent shoes or boots that would be suitable for riding.

They took advantage of the brunch specials at Dewey's, ate quickly and drove out to James's parents' ranch. The Brodys kept two older cow ponies, so all three of them couldn't go riding at the same time, but that was okay with Wyatt. He could ride whenever he wanted, at any number of places near his home. To Louise and Cassie, especially, staying in Texas was a unique adventure. Both women were accustomed to much larger towns. They probably wouldn't choose to live someplace like Brody's Crossing, but for a short while it was entertaining to be here.

James and his wife, Sandy, were there, along with his parents. While the guys saddled the horses, the women chatted about what was going on in town. Soon Cassie was up on her first Texas cow pony, a dun mare with a graying muzzle, while James rode alongside her on the other horse, a bay gelding.

"When are we leaving?" Louisa asked Wyatt as Cassie rode around the pasture.

"I don't know. I want to see about getting some decorations up along Main Street, but I'd need to get that approved by the city and I can't do that until Monday. We'll have to call the decorator and see if he has anything suitable. And then I guess we can get back to Carmel."

He didn't miss his house as much as he missed that darned cat. They had a bachelor roommate agreement of sorts, where they sat around, watched the ocean from the balcony, checked out sports on television and didn't ask too many questions about one another's comings and goings.

"Cassie and I can coordinate with the decorator as soon as we get approval."

"I'll take care of that." He thought about getting Toni involved somehow, if only as a liaison with the city manager. He could go by the hotel site on Monday and get to see how the demo was going, then drag her away to city hall. She probably wouldn't like having her orderly Monday disrupted, but heck, it would be good for her. Her life was too structured, even if she was busy and on a deadline.

Was she writing *have fun* into her planner anywhere? He doubted it.

James's father walked over and asked, "Are you staying to watch the game on TV? It starts around three o'clock."

"I guess so, if Cassie and Louisa don't have anything else planned."

"Caroline mentioned something about seeing if the ladies would like to go to the Christmas bazaar this afternoon. She and Sandy wanted to go."

"That would be fine with me. I need to buy some gifts and I haven't had time to shop," Louisa said.

"Okay, then." Wyatt motioned for James to bring Cassie around this way. When she got to the fence, she was grinning.

"This is so much fun. Is it time to go?"

"No, but Mrs. Brody wanted to know if you and Louisa would like to go with her and Sandy to the Christmas bazaar this afternoon, while the guys watch the Cowboys game."

"Sure. Do I need to get off the horse now?" she asked, reaching down to pat the old girl's neck.

"Not unless you want to, as far as I'm concerned," Mr. Brody said. "They're not leaving for at least thirty minutes. The bazaar is at the church in town, so it won't take long to get there and back."

James dismounted and helped Louisa up for a quick ride.

He watched with Wyatt from the fence. "They're nice. Cassie seems so young."

"I don't know her too well. She works for my assistant, Brian. She's actually twenty-six and has an MBA from Cal-Berkeley."

James nodded. "She really likes horses."

"What's not to like about horses? I wish my folks still kept some, but I know they don't want to fool with stock."

"Yeah, they can be a lot of work at times. Still, my father enjoys having a few cow ponies, some cows and a flock of chickens around the place. So, who's going to win today?" James asked.

"The Cowboys, of course," Wyatt answered. "Want to bet on the point spread?"

"No, not with you. I probably couldn't afford it."

James made the comment with a smile, but Wyatt wondered if everyone felt that way. Had his money come between him and his old friends? He'd never thought so, but maybe they did. Maybe his departure and his absence from town had made the gap between his good fortune and their choices seem much wider.

"Come on, Brody. Just because I have more money now doesn't mean I make crazy bets. But if you'll go get the beer, I'll pay for it."

"That's a deal."

AFTER THE WOMEN LEFT for shopping, Wyatt waited all of five minutes to call Toni on her cell phone.

"What are you doing?" he asked.

"Making sure I have all my subcontractor insurance certificates for the hotel project."

"Wow. Doesn't that sound exciting? If you can pull yourself away from that on a Sunday afternoon, come out to the Brodys' ranch. We're just sitting around watching football."

"We, as in you and James's parents?"

"James and Sandy, his parents, Cassie and Louisa. We came out to ride horses, but the ladies went to the Christmas bazaar for a while. They'll be back soon."

"I appreciate the offer, but—"

"Don't tell me that working on Sunday is more fun than watching the Cowboys win."

Toni had really liked football when they were younger. She'd gone to every game at B.C.H.S. when he was quarterback and James was his favored receiver. Wyatt remembered curling up on his couch or hers to watch the regular NFL season and playoff games. She could discuss the merits of zone defense and lament the Cowboys' propensity to call a short pass play on third and ten. Yes, those were some good times.

"There will be beer," he said, as if that would tempt her to drive out here. "And snacks."

He heard a big sigh on the other end of the phone, then some papers rustling. "Make it cheeseburgers on the grill at halftime and you've got a deal."

"Yeah? Okay. I need to see if the Brodys have ground beef." And a functioning grill, and condiments and cheese.

"I'll bring enough for burgers for eight people, right?"

"Right. Don't forget the buns."

"I won't. I'll be there before the end of the first quarter."

"See you then."

Wyatt grinned as he slipped his phone into his pocket. Toni was coming out for the game. For the afternoon. He really hadn't thought there was a chance that she'd take him up on his offer, but he was intent on trying to get her to have fun.

All work and no play made Toni a... Hell, she was still a smart sexy lady, no matter if she worked too hard or not. He simply didn't think devoting oneself to work was a good idea. Play had always been an essential part of his creative process.

He would rather have Toni to himself, to explore the attraction that still existed after fifteen years. However, since she was so reluctant to be alone with him, this way, at least they could be together in a group. Just like old times, in a way. Different friends, except for James. Different personal situations. But together, and that was something.

He strode out of the kitchen into the family room. "Hey, Brody. Er, James, that is," Wyatt added when Mr. Brody turned to look at him. "Fire up the grill! Toni's on her way."

Chapter Eight

Toni knew going out to the Brodys' ranch was crazy, but it also sounded like a great reason to avoid doing more paperwork, which seemed to be the case more and more of the time these days. Sooner or later, she was going to have to hire some office help, or maybe even a project manager.

She stopped by the grocery, said hello to her mother, who was working today while her father was home with Leo watching football, and got her customary generous discount on lean ground beef, buns, cheese, lettuce, tomato and onions. She figured the Brodys must have mustard and mayo. She'd done this before, picking up food for an impromptu cookout. Sometimes they'd gone to James's house, sometimes to hers and rarely to Wyatt's.

His mother didn't do well with "impromptu." Toni used to think that it was her; she'd assumed Mrs. McCall didn't want her dating her son. But then she'd realized that Wyatt's mother was just like that. Nothing around Brody's Crossing was good enough for Wyatt. His clothing, boots, school supplies and everything had come from Fort Worth or at a minimum, Weatherford. Mrs. McCall made frequent shopping trips to bigger cities, each time bringing home a carload of "stuff," as Wyatt called it.

Only toward the end of their senior year did Toni hear rumors of why Mrs. McCall needed an excuse to go off and shop elsewhere. "She has a problem," was whispered around town, especially after one of Wyatt's teachers got a slurred tongue-lashing from his mother for criticizing his behavior.

"This isn't about the past," she told herself as she drove out to the Brody ranch. She was looking forward to seeing Sandy and James, Mr. and Mrs. Brody. Wyatt would surely be on his best behavior around his employees and friends. Toni could relax and have fun. For a while, at least.

And then, there was the fact that Wyatt was probably leaving town tomorrow. There was no reason for him to stay. He'd completed his project and could report to everyone that his sentence had been served, above and beyond the official requirements.

When she arrived at the house, she pulled around back to unload her groceries near the kitchen. Wyatt was out on the patio, firing up the grill.

"You barely made it in time for the second quarter."

"Sorry. Shopping always takes longer than I think."

"I'll have the grill ready at halftime."

"Good thinking. I'll make the patties."

He turned to her and smiled. "We're still a good team."

"Hah. At the grill, maybe." He couldn't know how much his words hurt. They'd never been a good team. Teammates didn't run out in the middle of the game. "I'm going inside to say hello to everyone and get started on these burgers."

"I'll be right in."

Luckily, he seemed unaware of the sting of his comment. She opened the sliding-glass door and took the bags into the kitchen, which she remembered well. She'd been to the Brody house a few times over the past fifteen years. From the family room she heard the sounds of the game and the cheering of James and his father.

Caroline Brody, Sandy, Louisa and Cassie returned from the church Christmas bazaar as Toni was making hamburger patties. They put down their purchases, washed their hands and began slicing tomatoes and onions and tearing lettuce. The bazaar was well attended, they said, and already fairly picked over, so they hadn't stayed long. Soon Caroline shooed Toni off to watch the rest of the second quarter.

She stood there watching the punt to the Cowboys with five minutes, forty seconds left before the half, wondering where to sit. There was the couch and a rocking chair she remembered Mrs. Brody always using.

Wyatt didn't have any qualms. He walked into the room, smiling, a longneck in each hand, and gave her one. She took it automatically, as if she and Wyatt did this every day, then watched him plop on the couch as if he were eighteen still. He stretched out his long legs. "Have a seat, Miss Mayor. Watch the game."

She looked around, but Mr. Brody was lounging in his recliner and James and Sandy were draped across the two huge pillows on the floor. Toni sighed as she looked at the couch, and then sat down on the far cushion from Wyatt. While a Coors commercial played on TV during the change from the Cowboys special team to offense, he turned and looked at her, looked at the cushion between them, as if he knew she didn't want to sit close.

Too much like old times. Way too many memories…except back then they didn't drink beer. At least not in front of family. Maybe this had been a bad idea.

Her heart began to race and she felt flushed. Yes, this was a very bad idea. What had she been thinking?

WYATT LEANED FORWARD—and sideways, toward Toni—to put his longneck on the coffee table. "I don't have cooties," he taunted softly. "You don't have to hug the arm of the sofa."

"Grow up," she snapped under her breath.

"Where's your adventurous spirit?" he whispered.

She glared at him and turned her attention back to the screen. Adventurous spirit, indeed. He'd been the one set on danger. She'd just gone along sometimes for the ride.

Even back then, he could get her to do things that she knew weren't right. He hadn't changed, but now she had more willpower. Still, how could he upset her with just a look? A glance? He didn't have to *get* her in trouble to make her feel as if he had.

The five minutes of game time lasted over ten with penalties and time-outs. Toni felt as if she'd been sitting there forever. All she wanted Wyatt to do was get up and go grill the burgers, but the Cowboys had to settle for a field goal attempt and he wasn't leaving until he found out if they scored.

As they put three points on the board and time expired in the first half, everyone cheered. Mr. Brody and James got up. "We'd better put those burgers on," James said.

"I'll help," his father offered.

"I've been a slug. I'm going to see if I can help Caroline, Cassie and Louisa in the kitchen," Sandy said, stretching her petite body after sitting cross-legged on the floor cushion.

That left Toni and Wyatt alone.

She told herself to settle down and took a long drink of beer. The stuff didn't even taste good to her, but it gave her something to do. Her short nails drummed against the cold glass.

"You're supposed to be relaxing," Wyatt chided before she could jump up to go into the kitchen with the rest of the women. "Sundays are a day of rest, especially during football season."

"I'm trying to relax, but you— Oh, never mind. You always look at me as if you already know what I'm going to say. What I'm thinking. How can I relax around a know-it-all?"

"First, I'm not a know-it-all. I'm a know-a-lot. Second, you have a very expressive face. I know what you're thinking because you're showing your feelings."

She felt indignant. "I'm very good at hiding my feelings. I've worked damned hard to be peaceful and serene, even when there's high drama on the job site or in the council chamber." She took another drink of beer.

"Well, it's not working on me. You're like an open book."

Toni felt tears well up for no reason. No reason at all. "You mean a well-read book. An old book. A book you already know, but you read it anyway. The plot and characters aren't exciting anymore, but they're still there to read. I'm that kind of book to you, aren't I, Wyatt?"

He sat there staring at her as if she had lost her mind.

And then she did the absolute unthinkable. She ran out of the room, out of the front door, tears filling her eyes.

By the time she turned the corner of the house, she realized she didn't have her keys. They were in the kitchen, next to the grocery bags she'd brought inside. She kept on going at a fast walk, skirting the patio and grill, where James and Mr. Brody were dealing with burgers and cheese slices, and headed toward the barn.

She could find some quiet there. Solitude. That's what she needed to regain her composure. She opened the door and slipped into the dark, quiet, sweet-smelling haven of hay and grain and horses. Her eyes took a moment to adjust to the dim interior. There was a wide center section and stalls on one side, pens and a tack room on the other.

She'd been an absolute ninny, as her grandmother used to say, nearly crying in front of Wyatt. Bursting out about old books. Boring books. She rubbed her burning eyes and paced the length of the barn. Where had that analogy come from? She wasn't boring and she wasn't old.

She'd be boring to him, though. Wyatt McCall, one of the world's most eligible bachelors and most beautiful people. What was she thinking, accepting an invitation to watch football, grill burgers and drink beer with him? She didn't know how to relate to him now any more than she'd known how to keep him fifteen years ago. He'd dropped her fast and hard when he had the chance to leave town for the excitement of Stanford, never looking back. Probably not even remembering her amid the novelty of his new life.

And yet, he seemed to know her so well...

He definitely knew how to push her buttons. All of them. Her anger, her passion, her more vulnerable emotions. She sank down on a bale of hay outside one of the stalls. She wished she could blame the beer, but she'd drunk less than a full bottle. She wasn't that much of a lightweight, even though she didn't often drink anything stronger than white wine.

Politics and drinking didn't mix. She'd never been tempted to imbibe too much. She'd never been tempted to kiss men in her office, either, or lie with them in fake snow on the lawn of the community center. "Snow angels," she muttered. It was a wonder the security guard had believed Wyatt. Or maybe he hadn't and was simply too polite to say anything. At least he was a hired guard and not an off-duty Brody's Crossing officer.

She wasn't sure if she would run for mayor again, but she darn well wasn't going to disgrace the office by getting caught in a compromising situation with her ex-boyfriend. She was the figurehead for the town she loved, the town she worked so hard to improve, and she was going to do a fine job. Wild Wyatt McCall would be gone tomorrow, probably, and she wouldn't be tempted again.

He would leave and she would go back to her normal life. Why did that leave her with such an empty feeling inside? She should be happy that he was leaving her alone.

Alone.

"Toni?"

She heard the uncharacteristic hesitancy in his voice. She wasn't going to help him find her, but she wasn't going to run anymore. She should have controlled herself, laughed off his comments and focused on getting away from the Brody ranch as quickly and politely as possible.

"There you are," he said. She watched him walk toward her, backlit by the door, puffs of dust rising from his footsteps.

Without an invitation, he sat down on the hay bale, his momentum pushing her sideways. He looped his arm around her shoulders, keeping her from going anywhere. "What's wrong, babe?"

"I asked you not to call me that."

"Sorry. Old habits and all that."

"You can't have a habit that you haven't used in fifteen years."

"Sure you can, when it's something that seems so natural."

"You have a warped sense of what's natural, then. To me, it sounds degrading and way too familiar."

"You felt pretty familiar to me when I had my hand up your sweater and my tongue in you—"

"Stop it. You're just bored and it's easy to use me as your temporary amusement. Well, I'm not amused!"

She felt him tense. "That's cold, Toni, and it's not true that you're a temporary amusement." His tone was no longer playful. "I'm not some male chauvinist pig. I know you're a real person. I also know you're a beautiful woman."

She ignored his compliment and stuck to the facts. "I'm definitely temporary to you. Don't tell me you're staying longer than tomorrow. There's nothing to keep you here. You're finished with the project you didn't want to take on to begin with. You can get back to your real life. The beautiful house—yes, I saw it in a magazine—and the beautiful people and all the excitement."

"My life is more than a magazine spread."

He was probably right, but she didn't want to hear about how he'd arranged everything so that he could retire at thirty-three. She wasn't jealous or resentful, exactly. She just wasn't a part of his world and she darn well knew it. "You have the life you wanted, don't you? I'm not saying that you didn't work for it, but don't pretend that it isn't darn near perfect."

"I live in that beautiful house, which was decorated by and is maintained by other people, with a scruffy cat who barely tolerates me and a housekeeper I rarely see. It's true that my life is all about me, but that's not always a good thing."

"What do you mean?"

"Did you ever think about how overindulged I was as a kid?"

"Well…yes. Your mother thought you hung the moon and the stars. You were always her golden boy."

"That's not good for anyone, especially a kid who already had a big ego and a low threshold for boredom."

"You grew up okay. You survived your parents and none of your misadventures really hurt you or anyone else, thank heavens."

"True, I survived. I'm lucky."

"And talented. And smart. You were the boy who had everything."

"And yet I'm living alone with a cat. How pathetic is that?"

"Oh, please. Like I'm going to feel sorry for you."

"I don't want you to feel sorry for me. I want you to explain what I said to make you run out of the room. What happened, Toni?"

She sighed and looked at the beams, crisscrossing above their heads. "That was stupid of me. A temporary aberration. Let's just blame it on me being female."

"Oh, sure. You used to cut me to the quick if I made that kind of sexist remark. Besides, I don't believe you. You were genuinely upset and I'm trying to understand why."

"I've mellowed over the years. Besides, it's not sexist if I make the remark." She sighed and risked a glance at Wyatt. "Please, just go back to California. You made a wonderful display at the community center, attended your mother's dinner party and the chili supper in your honor, and now everyone loves you. You're finished here."

"You seem to want me gone awfully bad, babe. Why is that?"

She closed her eyes and took a deep breath. "I'm the mayor, not your 'babe,' as you so conveniently forget. I have a position to maintain in this town now, and you don't respect that. You don't care that part of my job is to inspire confidence in the office from the people whom I serve. Ever since you came to town, you've been trying to get me to compromise my position in town."

"That wasn't the reason I did…anything."

"I'm not going to argue with you about your intentions. I don't think you're *trying* to ruin my career. But, Wyatt, if you stay around here, that's exactly what you're going to do."

He removed his arm from her shoulder, then leaned forward and rested his forearms on his knees. The barn fell quiet, with only the scratching of some chickens and the snuffling of a horse in one of the stalls to break the silence.

"I'll make arrangements to get out of town tomorrow."

She took another deep breath. Okay, then. He was leaving. This was good. So why did she feel the sting of tears again?

"Just answer one question, now that I've agreed to leave you alone."

Alone. That word again. "All right. Which question?"

"Why were you so upset when halftime started?"

She didn't want to answer, but she owed him for granting her wish. He was leaving soon and things would go back to normal.

"Okay, I'll answer that one question." She jumped up from the bale of hay. She couldn't talk to him about her feelings while they sat so close together. She walked across the aisle and leaned against the tack-room wall.

"Most days, I don't think about you at all," she admitted. "As a matter of fact, I just about had myself convinced that I was over your sudden departure fifteen years ago." She took a deep breath. "And then I made that stupid remark to the reporter, which led to you coming back to town, and I had to see you all the time."

He looked as if he wanted to argue, but instead he said, "Go ahead."

"I guess I wasn't over your leaving so abruptly for college. I had to admit to myself—and now to you—that you hurt me. A lot. I've grown up and have my own life now, but there's obviously a part of me that is still eighteen years old."

"I'm sorry, Toni. I did what I thought was best at the time, in my own eighteen-year-old brain. I guess I didn't handle leaving very well."

"No, you didn't. But I think it also made the hurt worse because you deliberately didn't return. It was as if the first eighteen years of your life didn't exist. Or if they existed, they didn't matter." She took another deep breath. "That meant that I didn't matter. That I'd never mattered to you."

"High school wasn't all about me, was it? I mean, you were successful even back then. You were class president, homecoming queen and honor society. Everyone admired you. And of course you mattered to me. We had some great times together."

"And then you were gone," she said, not hiding the sadness she still felt. "You know, all those things you call successes for me paled in comparison to how I saw myself when I was with you. For example, I was only homecoming queen because you were the quarterback and the king. I know I did those things, but most people just saw me as your girlfriend. We were always together. We didn't date other people. You were the excitement and I was the common sense."

"You definitely had more common sense."

"Yes, but who got the better billing? You. The same with James, Tommy, Josh, even my little brother, Leo, and your other friends. We all looked to you as the leader. Every day was like, 'What's Wyatt going to do today?' You were a roller-coaster ride, Wyatt. We were all along for the ride."

"I think you give me too much credit. Or power. But that still doesn't explain why you got so upset today."

"I was getting to that. Okay, so you came back into my life, and I resisted being around you until I decided that was silly. I'm an adult and I could come to James's family home, just like we all used to, and enjoy the afternoon—especially after you taunted me with the fact I need to find time to have fun. So I came out here and, yes, it reminded me of the past. And then, when you said I was an open book, I remembered what it felt like when you discarded me so easily at eighteen. I remembered that I wasn't someone you wanted in your life at all. I was so boring, such an open book, that you had to go off and find new, more exciting people, places and things. I was the small-town past, and you were obviously destined for greater things."

"I didn't leave you because you were boring or because I knew you so well that you weren't exciting, or because I consciously thought about wanting new people or places."

"Oh? Well, it sure seemed that way to me. You barely said goodbye! You wouldn't even talk to me about your decision to go to Stanford early. That was what you were doing, and you didn't care if you hurt other people."

Wyatt sighed. "It's true that I didn't care enough about hurting other people. But to be totally honest, I did what I thought was best. For me, to be sure, but for you, too."

"How could running away from all we had have been the best thing?"

Wyatt got up and stretched, but thankfully he didn't try to walk over to where Toni still stood with her back to the wall. "Do you remember what happened the night of graduation?"

"Um, not really." She recalled a party after the official ceremony and the dinner with parents. She recalled feeling both mature and uncertain. She and Wyatt had probably gone off to "celebrate" as they usually did, in the bed of his truck, underneath the stars.

"Jennifer Hopkins got engaged to Tommy Wright that

night. Remember when they caught up with us at the lake? I'd never seen that look on your face before, babe. It was like you wanted to snatch that engagement ring right off her finger and put it on your own. Not that you weren't happy for her, I know. But you wanted that same thing. Jennifer and Tommy had been dating about as long as we had. You turned and looked at me as if to say, 'Where's my ring?' And I knew right then that I had to leave. Not just for me, but for you."

"How was that best for me? If you knew what I wanted, why didn't we talk about it? Why didn't you say that you didn't want to get married then? I wasn't expecting you to propose before you went away to college!"

"You don't understand," he said, walking slowly toward her. "I knew right then that you wanted to get married, that you expected us to get married, and that was the last thing I could do."

"I know we were just kids, but—"

"Not then, not now. Not ever," he said, as if she hadn't spoken. "It wasn't that I didn't want to marry you, babe. It was that I didn't want to marry anyone, ever. And that hasn't changed."

SOMEHOW, TONI MADE IT THROUGH the burgers and chips that were waiting when she returned from the barn. She claimed a whopper of a headache, which wasn't far from the truth, and left midway through the third quarter of the Cowboys game. Everyone was nice and solicitous.

Everyone but Wyatt, who had done an excellent job of avoiding her since *he* had returned from the barn.

Perhaps they'd said everything that needed to be said. She'd confessed why she'd run out of the house. He'd explained his reasons for leaving her so abruptly for college. Because he thought she wanted to get married. All because she'd been happy for Jennifer and Tommy. So happy. Such a perfect couple. They were still together, through sickness and health. Even their daughter Hailey's cancer, now in remission, hadn't separated them. If anything, they were closer now than they'd been at eighteen.

So close that there was little room in Jennifer's life for her former best friend. She had her own family. Toni accepted that, but she missed Jennifer and the girlish fun they'd had. At least she had her parents, and she saw Leo more often than ever since they were working together on the hotel project.

Toni sighed as she drove by her office. She couldn't face more paperwork. She had too much pent-up energy.

The odd thing was that she wasn't angry at Wyatt. Not at the moment, anyway. She'd found his confession sad and surprising. She needed some time to figure out why he'd decided never to marry.

Were his own parents so unhappy that they'd made Wyatt believe marriage wasn't worth the risk? She had no idea. The McCalls were very private people.

Toni rounded the corner onto Commerce, heading to the hotel job site. She pushed Wyatt out of her mind and walked through her project, which usually made her feel better. This was her largest renovation to date and it would go a long way toward securing her financial future, provided they could get the units sold or rented quickly. And if the retail space was also a success. She was hoping for a small restaurant, even one that sold prepared food and convenience items, similar to the all-purpose stores she'd seen in New York City.

And a coffee shop. Wouldn't it be great to have a place to go with friends for good coffee or tea? If no one else came up with the money or wanted to run it, she might have to take action herself. Find someone to manage it.

Since Wyatt was leaving tomorrow, she would soon have plenty of time to pursue her interests. No more "babysitting" his Christmas decorating project. No more worrying about what he would do next.

She'd gotten over him—sort of—once before and she'd get over him again. After all, nothing had really happened between them. A few kisses, some mild groping and a dash of heavy breathing. She'd done that much on some dates.

"Not in a long time," she reminded herself. Those would-be hot dates had been in college. Since then, she'd been too busy building her company and her political career. She couldn't date anyone locally because she couldn't take the risk of alienating voters. Everyone was either a voter or could influence people who were voters.

Which was how, at the ripe age of thirty-two, she'd had exactly one lover. Wyatt.

What would it be like to make love with a man? A full-grown mature male who could take his time, especially when she wasn't worried about getting caught. Sometimes, especially when she read a romance novel or went with her mother to a romantic comedy movie, she wondered. A lot.

Unless she made a weekend trip to Dallas or Fort Worth and trolled the singles bars, she wasn't going to find out. She absolutely couldn't risk getting involved with a man who might talk about her, especially if she wanted to split up and he didn't. Her reputation could be ruined so easily.

So, she might be permanently single. Perpetually celibate. Terminally frustrated.

Unless she did something bold.

Chapter Nine

Wyatt stretched out his legs on the king-size bed. He'd taken off his boots and changed into an old Stanford sweatshirt after coming back to the motel from the Brodys' ranch. Toni had left during the third quarter, but he'd put on a cheerful face and stuck around for the whole game. He'd even managed to laugh a little with the Brodys and tell Cassie and Louisa some stories about himself and James.

Now, though, he was alone. The two women had retired to Louisa's room to watch some estrogen-rich show, leaving him on his own. The television had basic cable channels, but he couldn't settle on anything. *Sunday Night Football* hadn't started yet and the news shows were either too depressing or too touchy-feely.

Especially after his conversation with Toni.

He supposed their talk had been a long time coming and was inevitable if they were going to be around each other for any period of time. He'd just ignored that possibility and focused on the fun aspects of being with Toni. Hell, he'd practically made it his mission to *make* her have fun.

Well, he should have left well enough alone. He should have told himself that he was only in town temporarily, to accomplish a goal, and then he'd be back to his life in California.

Except his life had changed since he'd sold his company.

He no longer had daily responsibilities for product development and marketing decisions. He didn't hire or fire people. As a member of the board of directors and creative consultant, he was still expected to target trends and see possibilities in future software applications, but that was more about thinking than doing.

He had all the time in the world to pursue whatever he wanted, yet he had no idea what to do. Keeping busy wasn't a problem; getting bored was. Always had been with him.

He was just about to flip through the channels again when he heard something hit his west-facing window. Was the wind that high? The day had been remarkably pleasant, perfect for horseback riding and grilling. Perfect for long talks with your ex-girlfriend about what a jerk you'd been way back when. And probably still were, from her perspective.

He heard the sound again. Maybe he should find The Weather Channel. See if a norther was coming through. That could mess up the plans he had to make sooner or later about getting back to California.

A decidedly louder "thump" hit the window, sounding less like wind and more as if someone was throwing something at his room. That seemed like a prank he might have pulled as a kid.

He swung his legs off the bed and walked to the door, opening it quietly. The walkway and parking lot faced south, with a tall single light near the road. His Hummer was fine, as well as the other cars in the lot. He stepped out onto the concrete, past the brightly painted vintage metal chairs provided for sitting outside, and headed for the corner of the building.

"Psst," he heard as he reached the corner.

He looked down the slight hill to the side of the motel and saw Toni squatting in the bushes. She wore dark clothing and her hair was pulled back under a cap. Her white sneakers made her look like part jogger, part cat burglar.

"What the hell are you doing here?"

"Are you alone?" she said in a loud whisper.

"Of course I'm alone. Why are you out there? In the dark."

"I didn't want anyone to see me. I couldn't just park in the lot and walk up to your door. I was sure Louisa or Cassie or any number of people might just pop their heads out of their rooms and see the mayor approaching the room of her ex-boyfriend. How would that look?"

"We have these great inventions now called phones."

"I wasn't about to call the motel and ask for your room. I, er, deleted your number from my cell phone when I was angry with you."

"Today or one of the many other times?"

She glared at him, which was rather comical given her position between two boxwoods. "I wanted to see you, okay? But maybe I'm changing my mind." She started to get up.

"No! Do you want to come in?"

"I'm fairly certain that if I do, I'll get caught. It's happened every single time. Louisa or Cassie or the night watchman. Maybe there will be a fire alarm. A meteor will strike the motel. Something horrible will happen, I just know it."

"Then what? Why are you here, if you're so certain something terrible will happen?" Why was she risking her reputation when they'd already had their "talk."

She sighed. "Because I had to."

"Okay, I have to hear this one. Do you want to go someplace else? Your house, maybe?"

"No! I can't have anyone see you come inside my house this late at night."

"It's not even eight o'clock yet."

"Shh! The sidewalks roll up early on Sunday night. You remember that, don't you?"

"Yes, I suppose so." He leaned against the corner of the building. "So, what did you have in mind?"

"Call Cassie and Louisa and tell them you're turning in early. Tell them you have a headache or something."

"That is such a girly excuse."

"Well, think of something!" Toni hissed.

"Okay, then what?"

"Follow me around the side of the motel. I parked my truck in back of the old rock house on that vacant property next door."

"Then what?"

"I thought we might…go for a drive," she said, her voice suddenly tense. "You know, like old times."

"Old times. Er, Toni—"

"Okay. If you don't want to go, just say so." He heard the bushes rustle as she duckwalked backward. "God, this is so humiliating." That statement was followed by an "umph" as she apparently stumbled or hit something. Probably went down on her butt.

"Wait, I want to go. For a drive. Whatever. Let me get my phone so I can call Cassie and Louisa. And a jacket. It's getting cooler."

"You're darn right it is. Hurry up, please."

"I'm hurrying. Do you want to come inside?"

"No," she snapped. "Listen carefully. I do not want to get caught!"

"Okay, got it. I'll be right there."

He couldn't wait to hear what she had to say. See where she wanted to go for a drive.

He quickly called Louisa's room and discovered both women were still watching their show. He said he was turning in early because he had a slight stomach ache from eating too many burgers and didn't want to be disturbed. That wasn't true; he hadn't eaten much since his appetite had deserted him after confessing to Toni. But his employees seemed to believe him.

So far, so good. He shoved his feet into some running shoes, then grabbed his phone and leather jacket. Tonight reminded him of old times. He and Toni, slipping around, out for a drive. Up to no good, usually because of something *he* had planned. This time, she'd taken the initiative. What did that mean?

Reevaluating his needs for the night, he went into the bathroom and fished around for more supplies. Better safe than sorry.

He grinned as he pulled the door shut. He was no longer bored.

TONI DROVE AWAY FROM the vacant lot with her lights off, just in case anyone saw her lurking about. She almost told Wyatt to bend down, but that would have been overkill. There was nothing wrong with her driving around with a passenger.

Of course, there was no one on the street after eight o'clock on Sunday night, she reminded herself as she switched on the lights and pulled out onto the road. The church people had already gone home from six-thirty services. All the businesses were closed here in town. The evening was quiet.

So quiet, she could almost hear her heart pounding. She glanced to the left, where the Christmas display was still on at the community center. The multicolored ornaments glowed on the bed of fake snow. She could still feel the softness of that snow, the hardness of Wyatt as he pressed against her. Thankfully, the inside of the truck was dark and he couldn't see her flushed face.

"So, where are we going?" Wyatt asked as she drove past her house on Elm Street.

"Um, well, since you're leaving tomorrow, I thought we might drive out to the scene of your original crime. Of course, if you'd rather not…"

"No, that's fine with me," he answered, stretching out his arm along the back of the seat. "It's kind of dark."

"There's at least a quarter moon, and the night is clear.

Now, since the tower is *white,* as it should be, it can be seen okay." Besides, she didn't really want to look at the stupid water tower. She wanted to look at Wyatt.

"I kind of liked it purple and gold."

"Don't even think about it." She stopped at the intersection of Commerce and Elm before continuing west.

He laughed and she relaxed just a little. "How many times do you think we drove out here?"

She tensed up again. So, he was thinking about…that. "I don't know." As the houses thinned out, the road curved and went up a rocky hill. The water tower was on the other side, high on the mesa off a dirt road.

"Nice pickup," Wyatt commented.

"What?" He knew she was picking him up? Like a desperate woman in a singles bar?

"Yeah, I like the extended-cab models. I imagine it's convenient for your work crews."

"Oh, yes," she said, breathing a sigh of relief. He was talking about her truck. "My work crews. Yes, it's absolutely essential." She drove slowly up the curving road, which cut around big red rocks and scruffy mesquite trees. She hadn't been up here in the dark in many years. The one time she'd come without Wyatt had been in broad daylight with the city manager and public works supervisor, when they were talking about repairs to the tower.

She pulled to a stop up high, between the water tower legs and the small concrete-block maintenance building. Her truck should be hidden from anyone driving around below, although she couldn't imagine why anyone would be out here at night.

Unless, of course, they were also up to no good.

"Do you want to let the tailgate down and look at the stars?" she asked Wyatt.

"Sure. I haven't seen the stars in the Texas sky in a long time."

"I imagine they look exactly the same as in California."

"You never know," he said as he opened the passenger side door. The light illuminated his smiling face.

That man was way too good-looking. Way better than the boy she'd known.

They shut the doors and walked around back. The rear of the truck faced the valley below, away from the town. Ranches and government land stretched out for miles, much farther than they could see in the dark with only a quarter moon for light. Toni unlatched the tailgate, put her hands on the cold metal and jumped up.

"I'm surprised you don't have one of those camper shells over the back," Wyatt said as he boosted himself onto the tailgate beside her.

"I would, except I sometimes transport appliances or other tall items in the back. Besides, I have a locked tool chest bolted to the bed of the truck. That's usually all I need."

"The thought of you with power tools turns me on."

Toni laughed. "You wouldn't say that if you saw how grubby I get sometimes."

"Sure I would. Besides, I've seen you grubby before. I don't remember that being a turnoff."

"Wyatt, you were eighteen. Nothing was a turnoff back then."

"You think I've changed?"

"I imagine you're more sophisticated now," Toni said, swinging her legs. She looked out onto the landscape. Very few houses were visible from here.

"I'm a guy. We don't mind sweat and a little dirt."

"I'm a girl. I like showers and shampoo that smell like flowers."

He leaned over and fingered a strand of her hair. "Hmm, you do smell like flowers."

"Disappointed I'm not covered in sawdust?"

"Not really," he said, leaning even closer, until his hot breath raised goose bumps along her neck. "I like girly-girls, too."

He kissed her just below her ear, making her close her eyes and sigh. Wyatt had always known just where she liked to be kissed. Touched. Did he remember? She thought he must, from when they'd kissed—and more—this past week.

She turned her head and found his lips in the dark. His arms closed around her and pulled her sideways, half across his lap.

"Wait," she whispered as she broke away. "I can't bend that way." Her legs scrambled for traction on the tailgate.

"How about this way?" he asked against her lips as he leaned back and pulled her with him. He kissed her deeply, his hands threaded through her hair. She felt light-headed, oxygen-deprived as the kiss went on and on.

Finally he broke for air, panting. "This metal is hard. Do you have blankets?"

"Um, yes." She reluctantly pulled away from his warmth and scrambled to her knees on the truck bed. She pulled two clean packing blankets from the tool chest, glad she'd remembered them earlier. When she'd thought about what kind of bold moves she might make while she had the chance.

Suddenly his warmth was against her back. He kissed her neck again as she knelt against the tool chest. Her fingers grasped the blankets as he rubbed against her. "You look and feel even better than you did when you were eighteen," he said. "I swear, the first time I saw you sitting behind your desk, I couldn't think of anything but what you might be wearing. On your legs. You have terrific legs."

"Um, thank you," she whispered, as his hands moved from her shoulders down, around her sides and toward her breasts. *Yes, touch me there,* she wanted to say.

His hands closed over her as if they'd been doing this forever. Thankfully, she'd worn a soft, lacy bra instead of something more practical. She could feel his fingers seeking, finding her sensitive nipples through the two layers of clothing. She moaned as he rolled the tips between his thumb and forefinger.

"We need those blankets. Now," he said against the side of her neck. "We may be acting like teenagers, but the bed of this truck is damn hard on my old knees."

That wasn't the only thing that was hard, she thought as she brushed against him once more before lifting the blankets the rest of the way out.

"You came prepared," he said as they spread one blanket on the truck bed. "I like that in a woman."

"Speaking of prepared, does that mean…"

"Yes, I came prepared also. Not that I assumed we'd do anything, but a guy can hope."

"That's okay. I don't have… Well, the mayor can't very well go into the drugstore and buy condoms." She shivered in the night air, now that Wyatt wasn't pressed against her.

"I don't suppose that would be a good political move." He tugged on the last corner of the blanket, then shrugged out of his jacket. "Come here, Miss Mayor, and I'll warm you up."

Yes, he would. They knelt facing each other, then he kissed her again and they sank slowly to the soft, thick blanket. Wyatt flung the other blanket over them as they tangled arms and legs. He rolled on top and she welcomed his weight.

"We have too many clothes on," he murmured close to her ear.

"I know, but I don't want to let you go. Even for a minute."

He looked down at her, an odd expression on his face, until she realized what she'd said. "I mean to get undressed. You feel so good."

He kissed her again, at the same time lifting her sweater. He barely broke contact to lift it over her head. Then his fingers went to work on her jeans. She ran her hands up his sweatshirt, feeling his hard muscles and rapid breathing. This grown Wyatt was bigger, stronger. He was a man, no longer a lean and sometimes too-rushed eighteen-year-old.

At least, she hoped he wouldn't rush too much.

"Lift up," he said as he unzipped her jeans.

She gasped as he whipped off her underwear right along with the pants.

"Now, that's what I call efficient," he said, a smile evident in his voice.

"You're not playing fair," she said, reaching for his sweatshirt.

"I'm not playing at all. I'm serious about getting you naked as quickly as possible."

"Don't rush me," she complained, pulling off his shirt. She reached for his jeans. The top button was already undone. She ran her finger along the zipper.

"Now who's playing?" he asked, his breathing heavy.

She pushed him onto his back, and he took advantage of her position to unfasten her bra and pull it off. The second blanket shielded her from both the cool temperatures and his eyes. But not his hands, which seemed to be everywhere as she struggled with his jeans.

"You're making me nervous, babe," he said as she tugged on the stubborn zipper. He moved from under her, quickly took care of undressing and turned toward her once more. "Now, where were we?" he asked as he dropped a handful of condoms on the blanket nearby.

She closed her eyes and stopped breathing as he pressed against her. Oh, yes. That's exactly where they were. Naked and suddenly in a great hurry.

Some things didn't change in fifteen years. And some things were much, much better.

WYATT LAY ON HIS BACK, staring at the stars and wondering what had just happened. Technically, he knew. He and Toni had just had mind-blowing sex in the bed of her pickup truck. In December, in Texas. Beneath the infamous water tower.

But why? He knew he should have asked, but he really hadn't wanted to talk. The adage, Don't look a gift horse in the mouth, came to mind. If Toni wanted him enough to throw rocks at his window, engineer an escape from town and fry his brain with sex, who was he to question her reasons?

And yet, he couldn't help wondering what had happened between the third quarter of the Cowboys game and the I-can't-get-you-out-of-your-clothes-fast-enough experience they'd just shared.

She wasn't talking. She was breathing, though, as she lay across his chest. He'd pulled the blanket over them until just the top of her head, his neck and face were free. The night was cool, crisp and silent. They seemed to be the only people on earth.

He could stay this way all night. Or until she roused. She felt so damned good, all damp and warm and womanly, her thigh across his and her arm around his chest. Her breasts, fuller now, were soft against him. She smelled like flowers and good sex. Like Toni.

The memories weren't as good as the reality. Or maybe he hadn't let himself remember how they'd been together. If he'd thought about her too much, he might have tried to see her on the rare occasions when he'd returned to Brody's Crossing.

Despite what he'd joked about earlier in the week, a "same time, next year" kind of relationship, that wouldn't have worked with Toni. She was too focused, too serious. He was too flighty, too adventurous.

"You're awfully quiet," she said softly, her breath tickling his chest.

"I thought you were asleep."

"Not really. Just…drifting."

"Yeah, drifting. Me, too." That was as good a description as anything of the way he felt. Knocked off his foundation was more like it, but he didn't want to admit as much to Toni. At the moment he was content to hold her in his arms. Sooner or later, though, he knew he'd feel the urge to run.

He always did.

But not right now. "You know, I don't have any pressing business back in California. I could stay a few extra days. Maybe we could talk about more Christmas decorations for the streets."

He felt Toni tense before she responded. Her breathing changed. Slowly, her leg slid off his thigh. "Um, that's probably not going to work for me."

"What?" He'd offered to change his plans, maybe buy something really nice for her town, and she said no?

"I'm really busy, and besides, if you stayed around town we'd want to do…this some more. I'd get caught in a compromising situation sooner or later. Probably sooner. No, I just don't want to push my luck."

"Luck?" *What about us?* he wanted to ask before he remembered that there was no *us*. "What about this?" he asked, sweeping his hand down her back and pulling her close.

"Oh, this was great," she said. "Better than I remembered. But we both know we don't have a future, right? You're West Coast and I'm strictly small-town Texas."

"Yeah, but—"

"And like I said, I'm really busy. We have budget meetings, and I've got the old hotel project. All the other Christmas events are coming up. The Settlers' Stroll next weekend, the VFW Christmas party, the Dewey's Christmas party. I'm just going to be so busy I wouldn't have time to spend with you, anyway."

Suddenly he felt really irritated. Very naked. And a little bit…used. "So, what was this?"

"This was great. Thank you very much."

Thank you? Had she really said that?

Chapter Ten

"You just wanted to get laid?" he asked. He couldn't believe she'd just told him "thank you" after what they'd done together.

"Crudely put, Wyatt. I prefer to think of it as a special reunion event."

This wasn't like any reunion he'd ever been to before. "In any case, you don't want to spend more time with me?"

"You were clear that you didn't want a relationship."

"No, I said I didn't want to get *married*. There's a huge difference."

"Really? I guess I missed that point. To me, a relationship doesn't make sense if it's not going anywhere. At my age, I have to start thinking about things like that. I mean, maybe I want to get married and have a child. Or children. I can't waste time on relationships that aren't moving in that direction."

"So you're looking for a husband?" The idea really irritated him. No one had mentioned that Toni was dating anyone or interested in finding a husband. Or that her biological clock was ticking. She hadn't mentioned anything of the sort. He had the sudden urge to jump up and pace, except he was naked, it was cold and he couldn't very well walk back and forth on the rocky ground or in the truck bed.

"I haven't been, but maybe it's time," she said, sounding

thoughtful. "I've spent so much energy on my business and my public service that I haven't looked."

"You told me you didn't have anyone in mind," he said, mentally going through the list of single men he knew in the area. There weren't that many that he was aware of, but still, the idea made him itchy.

"No, I don't. But Texas is a big state. I'm sure there's someone out there who's just perfect for me," she said as she ran her hand down his chest.

He and Toni had been pretty darned perfect together fifteen years ago. And also just a short time ago, for that matter. If she kept rubbing him, she was going to find out that his recovery time wasn't that far off what it had been when they were teenagers.

But he didn't want to get married. He couldn't imagine having a family to come home to every single night, a wife who would never bore him and most of all, children who wouldn't be disappointed if he screwed up or had to go out of town or made any of the other mistakes parents made. He was much more comfortable flying off whenever the urge hit him, having no one to report to and especially no one he was responsible for.

After all, being responsible was his weak point. Everyone except his mother said so. The most responsible thing he'd done was come back to Brody's Crossing so he could start his foundation with a clean slate. And he'd only taken care of his past indiscretion under pressure. Sure, he'd felt good about providing the new Christmas decorations, but that was hardly the same as dealing with a family of his own.

And Toni was looking for a mate, a family of *her* own, not just a roll in the hay. Or in the bed of a truck.

"So, this is just about having a good time?"

"Right."

Despite his slightly foul mood and his opinion that he'd

been used for sex, his body didn't seem to understand. As Toni's hand traveled lower, he sprang to attention.

"Don't be upset," she said softly against the side of his neck. "We have tonight. Good memories, right?" She kissed him right at his collarbone, just as he liked. "You can go back home all free and clear of your past."

Free and clear. Right. He might be legally free and morally clear of the transgression of painting the water tower purple and gold, but he wasn't going to forget Toni. And now he had new memories that he was pretty sure would haunt his nights.

"I'll go back to California tomorrow, just like I promised," he said, framing her face with his hands and gazing into her eyes in the faint moonlight. "Just don't forget me when you're out looking for Mr. Right."

"I won't," she whispered. "You know damn well I won't." Then she pulled his head down and kissed him, and he forgot to feel anything but their passion for a long, long time.

TONI PULLED INTO HER DRIVEWAY after turning off her lights and coasted to a stop in front of the single-car garage she used for storage. Old Mrs. Olsen next door was a fairly light sleeper and Toni would hear about it if she disturbed her after midnight, especially "on the Sabbath," as her neighbor would say.

Toni glanced at the dashboard clock. Twenty minutes past one in the morning. She was going to be tired—and probably achy and stiff—all day.

She was going to be lonely and full of memories for a lot longer. She'd done what she'd wanted to do, but she would pay a high price. Wyatt would leave sometime today and life would go back to normal. Toni knew she wasn't going to go back to the way she'd been before he'd returned to town just last week. He'd made her think about what she wanted, what was important at this point in her life, and now she couldn't ignore her needs.

She wouldn't be fulfilling her wish list with Wyatt, but that was to be expected. They had little in common. They were at far different places in life. And as she'd learned at the Brodys' ranch less than twelve hours ago, he never wanted to marry.

She hadn't thought much about getting married until then. She'd focused so much attention on the future of Brody's Crossing that she hadn't had any time left over to think about *her* future. She'd also thought she was over the past, but she wasn't. Now she could seriously look at both issues—how much Wyatt had hurt her at eighteen, and what she wanted now at thirty-two—and go forward.

Well, she couldn't sit in her truck all night. She needed a hot shower and some warm flannel pajamas. Maybe some herbal tea. She smelled like Wyatt, ached as if they'd rolled around on a metal mattress and was far too wound up to sleep.

She eased the driver's-side door open and hoped the interior light wouldn't shine into Mrs. Olsen's bedroom. She manually clicked the lock and softly latched the door so the "beep-beep" of her key alarm wouldn't engage. Resisting the urge to walk on tiptoes, she climbed the three steps to the back door and let herself in.

There. She'd made it home without getting caught in a compromising situation with her ex-boyfriend. Good going. She and Wyatt had used condoms and that was responsible, and as far as she knew she had no marks to show that she'd spent the night making love under the stars.

No, *having sex* under the stars. They weren't in love and apparently he'd never been in love with her. She couldn't say the same about her feelings for him. Maybe it was better to have loved and lost, because she felt sorry that Wyatt didn't know what it felt like to love someone so much that it took more than fifteen years to get over that person.

On the other hand, he didn't have the burden of getting over someone who didn't love him back.

With a sigh, she pushed away from the door and went to her bathroom. Time for that shower. And just to be careful, she'd check to make sure Wyatt hadn't given her a little extra love bite as his way of saying goodbye.

That would have been so Wyatt-like, she thought with a sad smile.

TONI ARRIVED AT HER JOB SITE early that morning and kept busy despite her lack of sleep.

"Did you have trouble sleeping?" Leo asked. "You look bushed."

"Yes, I guess I did. Maybe I'm getting to that age where I can't drink any caffeine after six o'clock at night."

"Oh, man. That is getting old," he said, good-naturedly. "I'm glad I'm the younger brother."

"You're not that much younger. Four years gets less and less important as we get older."

"Still, big sister, I haven't turned the big three-zero yet, whereas you are officially over the hill."

"Gee, thanks for reminding me." She clipped her tape measure onto her work belt and looked at Leo. "That reminds me. I've decided that I'm going to try to work dating into my schedule. So, if you know anyone and want to fix me up with someone *decent,* just let me know."

"What's your idea of decent?"

"You know, no gross habits. Employed. Reasonably intelligent and good-looking. Pleasant and kind."

"That's a pretty big wish list, sis. Does he have to be older than you?"

She thought about it a moment. "Not necessarily, although I wouldn't want anyone more than a few years younger than me. Let's say thirty."

"Okay, then. You want a thirty-something Prince Charming who has a decent job, doesn't scratch his pits or burp in public, and likes puppies." Leo laughed. "Wait! I've seen that guy. It's your old boyfriend."

Toni punched her little brother in the arm. "Shut up, you dork. You're insane. I'd rather have someone who wasn't anything like Wyatt."

Leo looked at her closely. He sometimes irritated her, as any younger brother would, but Leo was sharp as a tack and had a special knack for reading people. "Really? Wow, that's an interesting comment."

"Is not. I just mean that I'm not trying to replace him. He's leaving town and I'm moving forward." Toni picked up her level and pulled a flat carpenter's pencil from her work belt. "Besides, don't you want to be an uncle someday? I'd better get busy meeting someone, if that's going to happen."

"An uncle? I think I'm too young for that kind of responsibility."

"You won't be by the time I find Mr. Right and manage to drag him to the altar," Toni muttered. Getting started on this dating thing was going to be harder than she'd anticipated.

After marking the height for the new wainscoting that would be put up this week, Toni went to work upstairs, assessing the plumbing needs in the bathrooms that were being created in each unit. The old baths had been completely removed, as they weren't original to the property. Back when the hotel was built, there were public baths on each floor. The only exceptions were the ladies' suites, with shared baths just for women, on a different floor.

Now the past had been swept away into roll-off containers and recycling bins. Of course, first they'd used hammers, mallets, saws and sweat to tear everything out.

Sometimes removing the past was painful. But it had to be done. Toni sighed and took a look at her parts list. She just hoped she could stay busy until Wyatt and his entourage got out of town. Until he removed himself, she couldn't start the equally difficult task of getting on with the rest of her life.

"SO, I HAVE INTERVIEWS SET UP with *People* magazine and *Us Weekly* West Coast correspondents," Louisa said. "Cassie is getting the details on when they'll be in Carmel. They both want photos of you at home, and I'm providing JPEG files of the Christmas display."

"Hmm," Wyatt said, sitting back in a soft butter-colored leather seat in the private jet he'd arranged for their trip back to California. Cassie and Louisa sat across the burled walnut table. The trappings were nice, but Wyatt felt as unsettled as if he were flying coach nonstop to Australia. Sitting next to a big guy with BO and a screaming baby.

Definitely itchy.

"Does this thing have any exercise equipment?" he asked.

"I… I don't know. I'll go check," Cassie answered, jumping up and approaching the attendant, who sat just behind the cockpit.

Wyatt wiggled in his seat. He must have the imprint of a Ford truck bed on his back. And butt. After what they'd done, he should be limp with satisfaction. In actuality, he was wired, as if he'd drunk an entire pot of black coffee, and frustrated, as if he hadn't just spent most of the night buried deep within a beautiful blonde.

He still couldn't believe Toni had taken him out to the water tower, used him for sex and sent him on his way. She really didn't want him around "her" town anymore. She'd made her reasons sound so rational. She'd used his words against him.

They couldn't have a relationship unless it was "going somewhere." That meant get married. Hah! He wasn't getting married. She was being unreasonable, no matter how reasonable she claimed she was being.

"Did you say something?" Louisa asked.

"Did I?"

"Um, I thought so, but maybe not." She paused and looked at him closely. "Is everything okay?"

"Just peachy." He unfastened his seat belt and bolted from the chair. If he could do no more than pace the length of the plane, that's what he'd do. He made it front to back and returned to Louisa's side.

"It's not you. I'm just in a bad mood."

"Yes, sir."

Cassie returned then. "I'm sorry, but there's no exercise equipment. There is a bed in the back, if you'd like to nap."

"No bed," he said, and began pacing again.

The last thing he needed at the moment was to get into a bed while he was still thinking about Toni. He'd be better off finding a parachute and jumping out of the emergency exit. No, he shouldn't think that way. He'd gotten into trouble more than once by imagining the most outrageous stunt he could perform without a high probability of serious injury or death.

"How about a game of cards?" Cassie asked. "My grandmother always suggested cards when we traveled, to keep us entertained."

Wyatt stopped and looked down at Cassie and Louisa, both of whom were obviously concerned about him. "Okay, let's try cards. I promise to play fair."

"We always think you're fair, Mr. McCall," Cassie said.

"I'm sorry you're...concerned about leaving your hometown. It seems like such a nice place," Louisa added.

"The horseback riding was really great," Cassie said. "Thank you very much for that."

"No problem. I'm glad I could do it." And despite how he felt, now that he and Toni were once again going their separate ways, he was glad he'd returned. The week hadn't been boring, that was for sure.

He paced until Cassie returned with some cards. Wyatt flopped back into his leather chair and broke open the deck. "Five card stud, deuces and jacks wild," he said, discarding the two jokers with a flip of his two fingers.

"Um, what?" Cassie said.

"I know how to play hearts and bridge," Louisa offered tentatively.

Wyatt laughed. "Just kidding, ladies. You pick the game. I'll try my best to play nice." He'd do almost anything to keep from thinking about Toni and how she'd discarded him as easily as he'd flipped those jokers out of the deck.

He looked at the two masked harlequin-costumed jokers lying on the floor. Who took jokers seriously?

Maybe it was time Toni understood that he was no longer playing the fool.

BRODY'S CROSSING Settlers' Stroll occurred the weekend after the first Saturday of December, since the first weekend was always reserved for the parade. The Stroll had been an annual event for as long as Toni could remember. When she and Leo were children, their parents had dressed them up in homemade costumes and people met at city hall. Now everyone gathered at the farmers' market, since it had a nice awning and lights. Most people kept their costumes from year to year, but some women sewed new outfits almost every Christmas for themselves and their families.

Since she was mayor, she started off the Stroll by visiting various businesses in the old downtown section. Proprietors offered hot drinks and yummy confections, and some gave small gifts to the children. Everyone had a great time socializing and imagining how Christmas used to be a hundred years ago, when Brody's Crossing was a young town in the still somewhat Wild West of Texas.

Tonight Toni wore her 1890s-style lady's walking dress,

which was really a light gray suit with a white blouse. Her hat only worked when the wind wasn't blowing too hard, since it sported a floppy brim and lots of silk flowers and peacock feathers. Instead of the horribly uncomfortable shoes the original settlers would have worn, she opted for sensible women's boots, knowing no one could see them anyway under the long skirt. Beneath the old-fashioned trappings, she wore high-tech thermal underwear and socks to keep her warm as she strolled. Corsets and thin cotton shifts couldn't compete with Gore-Tex.

"There," she said to herself in the mirror in the office hallway. She looked as she always did for the annual event, with her hair pulled back and wound into a chignon and her great-grandmother's jet bead and enamel brooch pinned to the lapel of her jacket. Little jet earrings dangled from her ears. She'd gotten dressed at home, then driven to her office. From here, she'd walk to the farmers' market.

Two high-school girls had been hired to serve refreshments at her office this year. This was the first time she'd ever opened her business to the public for the event. Now was the time to start thinking about the future, beyond being mayor, when she could concentrate more fully on renovation projects.

An artist's rendering of the railroad hotel project, created for the city council presentation by her architect in Fort Worth, was the focal point this evening. It was displayed prominently on an easel where everyone could see it as they entered the conference room for hot mulled cider and cookies. With any luck, she might meet some potential condo buyers or retail space renters tonight.

The two students she'd hired knocked on the door. "Come in," Toni called out. They entered on a gust of cool evergreen-scented wind.

She gave the girls instructions and showed them where everything was, pulled on her long calfskin gloves, then ventured outside.

She stopped next door at the hardware store and convinced her brother, Leo, to leave his own feast of imported chocolates and walk with her down Main Street, past the bank. Leo had dressed as a gambler in black and silver, rather like the old *Maverick* TV series their father watched. The choice was appropriate since, as Leo liked to say, he'd played a little poker in his day. Most people laughed, since Leo was only twenty-nine years old, but Toni's brother was a math genius and all card games came easily to him.

They crossed the street at Commerce and strode past the city hall and then Clarissa's House of Style. The big picture window was brightly lit and outlined in tinsel.

Which made Toni think of the somewhat pitiful and weathered tinsel-covered candy canes that the city placed on utility poles around town every December. Wyatt had mentioned replacing them, but she'd insisted he leave before he could take any further action.

After all, he'd done enough. Fulfilled his duty, completed his sentence and all that stuff. There was no reason for him to stay in Brody's Crossing or do anything else for the town. Thank goodness. Seeing him work on another project, or just knowing that he'd bankrolled more decorations, would make her think of him more.

She didn't need that burden. No, it was best that he'd returned to California, to his beautiful home and scruffy cat. He'd probably gone off on another adventure by now, possibly someplace sunny and tropical, or maybe someplace snowy and bright. Someone would probably show her a photo of him in a celebrity magazine next week, going somewhere exciting with yet another beautiful woman. The anticipation alone made her tense.

Toni stumbled on the uneven sidewalk. Leo reached out to steady her. "Hey, we should tell the city about these sidewalks. They're a real hazard," he said.

"Very funny," she said, turning right onto Market Street. The farmers' market was just across the road. "We have sidewalk improvements in the budget for next year, I'll have you know."

"And not a moment too soon," Leo said.

A group had already formed beside the structure, although it was another thirty minutes before the actual stroll was scheduled to take place. Toni liked to get there early to talk to people. They often opened up more in this casual environment than when she was sitting behind her desk at city hall.

She spotted Cal and Christie Crawford, who seemed to be without their son, Peter. He was probably home with his nanny, Darla Maxwell. Christie appeared very pregnant in her matching dress and long fur-trimmed coat. They were talking to James and Sandy Brody.

"Come on," Toni said to Leo. "Let's socialize with people we know best at first." They walked the thirty feet or so to where everyone was gathered.

"How are you feeling?" she asked Christie.

"Okay, although I'm a little more tired than I was with Peter. I'm excited about tonight, though. This is my first Settlers' Stroll. Hopefully, next year I'll need a different dress in a smaller size," she said, rubbing her hand over the mound of her stomach and giving Cal a look.

Toni smiled automatically, but she felt a twinge of envy, too. Soon Christie would have two beautiful children—after she'd once been told that she couldn't get pregnant. Boy, had that doctor been wrong! Still, Toni knew that every year over the age of thirty, a woman's chances of conceiving went down. She'd be thirty-three in January. Would she ever have a child? Did she want one? Or was her career and her service to Brody's Crossing enough?

The more she'd thought about it lately, the more she believed she wanted a family. Her mother and father would be fantastic grandparents, and if she had children they'd have an excuse not to work so hard at the grocery. And Leo would make a really fun uncle.

Damn Wyatt for making her think about her ticking biological clock! Before he came to town, she'd been blissfully unaware of what she was missing. Now, she not only thought about having a baby, but what you had to do to get pregnant.

She'd spent many nights this week tossing and turning, remembering their time together under the stars. She'd managed to convince him that she wanted nothing from him, but her body was screaming, yes, yes, yes!

"I'm really happy for you. I hope you have a good time tonight. If you get tired, though, just find a comfortable place and sit a spell and talk to whoever is around. That's what tonight is all about—meeting up with neighbors, old friends and new ones."

"Thanks. I'll remember that. See you later." Christie and Cal walked away, arm in arm.

"Hey, there's Mom and Dad," Leo said, nodding toward the couple in prairie attire, who were getting out of their sensible Chevy sedan in the parking lot behind the farmers' market. "Looks like they brought Myra Hammer with them."

"Oh, that's going to put Dad in a bad mood. Myra can be pretty critical of his driving."

"And everything else. Watch out or she'll blame you for the windy weather."

"I'll go say hello and then excuse myself. Maybe you should stay and talk to Mom and Dad while I go mingle. Officially, of course."

"I wish I had a good excuse."

"When my tenure is finished, *you* can always run for the job."

"You'll be mayor forever. You love this stuff."

Toni shrugged, then headed toward her parents. "Hi, Mom, Dad. You look great."

"I think my dress is tighter this year," her mother said,

fluffing the skirt. "I'm going to have to stop eating those day-old blueberry muffins."

Toni laughed. Being in the grocery business was both good and bad for her folks. Low profit margins, but plenty of leftover bakery items and slightly bruised bananas.

"At least the temperatures are nice tonight," her dad said.

"Bah! The wind's blowing too hard," Myra said.

"Sorry, but I've got to go mingle," Toni said. "I'll see you later," she told them. She thought she heard Leo moan.

The group had swelled as she'd been talking to her parents. Everyone seemed to be enjoying the visiting. Soon it would be time to start the procession. She really did have to mingle, so she waved to her parents and excused herself from the Crawfords and Brodys.

She walked to where Clarissa, Venetia, Ida Bell, Bobbi Jean and Burl Maxwell stood nearby. "How are you tonight?" Toni asked the group.

"Just fine, honey," Clarissa said, wrapping her wool shawl around her. Clarissa's generous bosom looked as if it might burst the buttons on her high-neck green dress. She was a widow who wasn't looking for a man, although she might get some attention in that dress.

"I wish Caroline could be with us, but she's back at James's law office again this year." Caroline Brody was one of their lunch buddies.

"And Rodney is with the 4-H Club. They're doing a fund-raising bake sale at the café," Ida said, explaining her husband's absence.

Toni knew so many of these families, most of them all her life. She looked around but didn't see Mr. and Mrs. McCall. They always attended, usually strolling with banker George Russell and his wife.

Just then, Toni heard the clatter of hooves. Not the tiny little reindeer kind, but horses coming down the street. Others must have heard them also, because the entire group of settlers turned back and forth to see where the sound was coming from. Suddenly, from the direction of McCaskie's Service Station, a stagecoach came into view, clattering around the corner and into the pool of light beneath the streetlamps.

"Whoa!" the driver called out, pulling the team of four to a prancing stop right in front of the farmers' market. The other man, the one with a shotgun Toni hoped was empty or a prop, climbed down and opened the stagecoach door. Both men were dressed in Western frontier outfits.

The McCalls climbed out, and then the Russells. The crowd clapped and gathered round. Toni held her breath, nearly expecting Wyatt to step out next. But he wasn't in there. Of course he wasn't. He was in California. Or Tahiti. Or on Mount Everest.

The last time she remembered Wyatt attending the Settlers' Stroll, he, James and several others had dressed up as "wild Indians," as the police chief had called them, and run up and down the line of settlers, whooping and hollering. Despite the cold weather that night, they'd worn only loincloths and war paint.

She sighed. Wyatt hadn't enjoyed the strolling part of the Settlers' Stroll; walking with friends and neighbors was far too tame. He'd only enjoyed disrupting the event. Since he swore he was now on his good behavior, why had she even thought that he might return?

Chapter Eleven

"What an entrance!" Toni heard someone say.

"Where'd you get that stagecoach?" someone else asked.

Toni made her way to the front after spotting Martha Chase talking to the driver. Martha coordinated the Settlers' Stroll with the public works director for the city. No one had mentioned a stagecoach during the planning meetings.

The group greeting the McCalls and the Russells moved away from the stomping, head-bobbing horses. Others looked on from a distance. Martha motioned for Toni to join her near the stagecoach.

"Isn't this great? We should have thought of this before," Martha said, whipping out her digital camera.

"*We* didn't think of it now," Toni answered. Apparently, the McCalls had really decided to get into the Old West spirit. She couldn't imagine stodgy George Russell coming up with anything so whimsical.

"Step up here and let me take your picture," Martha said.

"Really, I don't think that's necessary," Toni replied, gazing into the dark interior.

"No, no, I really want your picture. This will look great in the newsletter."

Toni resigned herself to being photographed in the stagecoach. "Okay, but hurry. We need to begin the stroll soon."

"Oh, of course," Martha said, fidgeting with her camera settings.

Just then another set of hoofbeats caught everyone's attention. Toni swiveled from her perch on one of the leather seats of the coach. A masked man rode down Market Street, waving another—hopefully—fake gun. He made his horse rear slightly. The crowd cheered.

"What's going on now?" she asked Martha.

"I believe our bandit is here."

"Martha, whose idea was this?"

But Martha didn't answer, stepping back as the bandit approached the stagecoach. Toni was trapped unless she wanted to step into the path of the nervous horse. "This is a robbery!" he shouted. "Hand over your Wells Fargo cash box." He brandished his gun as his horse pranced to the delight of the crowd.

Surely this little drama would be over soon. She leaned out the window to see more of what was going on.

"Well, well," the bandit said, his voice vaguely familiar although somewhat muffled by his bandanna mask, "What do we have here?"

"That's the mayor," a man in the audience shouted.

"The mayor! Why, I thought maybe she was the schoolmarm. She sure is a pretty lady."

"She sure is!" someone answered.

Toni felt her cheeks flush. Okay, now this was getting embarrassing.

"I'll take that cash box and the pretty lady," the bandit announced.

"Oh, no, you don't," she muttered, ready to get out of the stagecoach.

"Driver, follow my directions and no one gets hurt," the bandit shouted. He waved his gun around some more, then to Toni's shock, the stagecoach lurched forward and the door slammed shut. She heard the shout of the driver to the horses, the clacking of the wheels and the panting of the bandit's horse, just outside the window. Righting herself, she grabbed the door frame and stuck her head out the window.

"Okay, fun's over. Take me back," she ordered.

The bandit drew even with the coach as it followed the old road next to the railroad tracks. They slowed as they came to the intersection with Commerce Street. The streetlamps illuminated the man and his dark horse. "Sorry, pretty lady," he said, holding the reins in one hand as he pulled his bandanna lower with the other. "I sure can't do that."

She felt as if the air had been knocked out of her lungs. "Wyatt! What are you doing?"

"I'm abducting you. Tell me this isn't the most fun you've had at one of these events in years."

"Fun? You're embarrassing me."

"No, I'm not. The crowd loves it. And I'll take you back soon." The stagecoach slowed as they reached the old hotel construction site, then continued on to a vacant lot.

"Stop here," he told the driver.

The stagecoach came to a stop. Wyatt swung down from his horse and tied the reins to the back of the stagecoach. "Wyatt, I need—"

"No," he said, opening the door. "*We* need to talk."

Toni scooted over when it became obvious he intended to barge in. He had a lot of nerve, renting this stagecoach, planning an abduction and insisting she listen to him. Of course, Wyatt had always possessed more than his share of nerve.

Why else would he always risk so much?

What was he risking now? The question haunted her as she looked across the dimly lit interior of the coach. Only the streetlamp provided light so she could see his face.

"We won't be gone long, I promise. I had to do something dramatic to get you alone, since you've made it clear that coming to your house or your office might be seen as a clandestine rendezvous."

"Oh, and abducting me from the Settlers' Stroll isn't?"

"Of course not. We're still in public, albeit in a rather deserted piece of the downtown area. The driver is sitting up there," Wyatt said, pointing toward the roof, "and if you'll hear me out we'll simply make two turns and be back on Main Street in no time. We can catch up with everyone and you'll be greeted as the rescued damsel in distress."

"I've never been a damsel in distress. Aren't you mixing metaphors or something? You're not a knight in shining armor. You're a bandit dressed in black!"

"Okay, bad analogy. Anyway, just listen. I was really angry when I left town. I was a bear to everyone all the way back to California, when I got to my house and when I tried to concentrate on anything at my office. Finally, my assistant, Brian, strongly suggested that I take some time and resolve whatever was bothering me."

"I can tell you what's bothering you. Someone finally told you *no*. That must have been a first."

Wyatt shrugged, not denying her statement of fact. Wyatt had been a spoiled child, an arrogant youth and a cocky teenager. He'd also been kind, funny and charming.

"You never meant to hurt anyone," Toni admitted. "Never, even when you pulled your most outrageous stunts."

"As much as I'd like to agree with that praise, that's not exactly true."

"What do you mean?"

He took a deep breath. "It took me a lot of years and, I'll even admit, a few talks with a therapist, to understand that I was trying to hurt my parents. And punish myself."

"Wha-what?"

"I know most people didn't see it, but I had a lot of anger inside me, Toni. My mother… Well, she had her own problems, mainly that she's an alcoholic. I didn't see that as a disease. I saw it as a disgusting choice. I thought she was weak. I didn't like her or what she did. I resented her when she wasn't awake and aware for me, and I resented her when she was involved and overindulgent.

"Basically, my whole childhood was spent being angry at my mother, whether she slept through me doing something dangerous that she should have stopped or defended me when she should have swatted my bottom or at least given me the mother of all time-outs. And I was angry at my father for not stopping her, for failing to stand up to her. Lots of people had perfect parents, from my point of view. You, the Brodys, the Bells. I had a drunk mother and a weak father."

"Oh, Wyatt. I had no idea that's how you saw your childhood. I mean, I understood, when we were seniors, that your mother had a problem. But I didn't know that's how you felt."

"Yeah, I didn't know it at the time, either. This all came later, after I left Brody's Crossing. Once I was in college and there was no one to show off for, no one willing to defend me unequivocally, I felt lost."

Toni reached over and put a gloved hand over his tightly clasped ones. "I'm sorry there was no one there for you."

"No, it was best. I needed a break. I did leave town because I knew you wanted to get married." When she started to object, he cut her off. "No, don't get defensive. Maybe you didn't expect it right then, but I knew it. You loved me."

Toni looked down, unable to watch him as she admitted, "Yes, I did."

"And it was perfectly normal for you to think that we'd get engaged at some point in the next few years, and get married after we graduated from college and settle down like our friends and produce the two-point-three children or whatever."

She nodded.

"I'm not saying that was unreasonable or unexpected. I'm trying to explain, which I didn't do a very good job of when we talked a week ago, that I panicked whenever I thought of being married. Of being with one person who had that much control over my happiness. I didn't realize why until long after I left for college, when I talked to someone—finally—about my resentment."

"But if you resolved your feelings, why not take a chance with someone? Lord knows, you've taken chances on almost everything else in your life. Your education, your business, your adventures. And surely you've met a lot of wonderful women, even if I do resent most of them for being so beautiful and talented."

"I can understand how you'd think that because I understood my issue, I was over it, but old habits die hard. Whenever I thought of being with someone forever, I got what I can only describe as an itchy feeling. It's like I need to move, run, go. Like I'm someplace I don't want to be and the only thing to do is get myself someplace else. Anyplace else. That's not a good thing, when you're talking about commitment and children and all that."

"No, it's not," Toni said, and sighed. "So, where does that leave us? Nothing has really changed. Why did you come back if you still feel that way?"

"Because," he said, disengaging one hand and cupping her jaw, "I discovered that I felt itchy when I *wasn't* with you." Then he leaned forward and kissed her, gently. An awakening kiss like he hadn't given her since they were teenagers first experimenting with simple touches of their lips.

He leaned back slightly and looked into her eyes. "I'm just asking for a chance, Toni. I'm not perfect and I'll still make mistakes, but can we try?"

"Try what?"

"Having an adult relationship."

"I... I don't know. I have to think, and I've never been able to think when you're so close. You overwhelm me, Wyatt."

"I don't mean to."

"I know," she said softly, "but you do, and that's something I have to come to terms with before we can go forward."

"But you'll try?"

"I promise."

He smiled, which seemed to light up the stagecoach interior. "That's all I can ask. For now."

She took a deep breath and leaned back. "We'd better get back to the Settlers' Stroll."

"You're right. I have to make sure the pretty lady mayor's reputation isn't tarnished by the bad bandit."

"That would be appreciated."

He kissed her quickly once more, then swung down from the door. Within seconds he was mounted and riding away, the stagecoach lumbering after him. And a few minutes later they'd pulled to a stop in the middle of Main Street, in front of her office.

Wyatt, who had replaced his bandanna mask, opened the door with a flourish for the strollers, who had begun to gather.

"Even I, a lowly bandit, cannot rob such a paragon of the community. Such a beautiful and gracious lady. So I return her to you." He reached down, kissed her gloved hand and swept his cowboy hat in a courtly bow. Then he was off, mounting his horse.

The nervous animal pranced as Wyatt shouted, "Until we meet again, fair citizens! Beautiful lady!" He galloped away, some giggling children running after him.

Toni stood in the middle of the street, stunned, as people walked up to her. She watched as the bandit disappeared from sight around the corner, out of the streetlamps' pools of light.

Itchy. Now she understood. She was feeling it, too.

WYATT GAVE THE OWNER-DRIVER of the stagecoach a generous tip after he loaded the last horse back into the trailer. The stagecoach had been rolled onto a flatbed and secured. The driver's sidekick was also the driver of the truck pulling the flatbed back to Weatherford.

"Drive carefully," Wyatt said with a wave as they pulled out of McCaskie's parking lot. With the last of the settlers still strolling downtown, he was finished for the night. Time to check into the motel.

He'd reserved the same room again. This time he'd come to Brody's Crossing alone, without Cassie or Louisa. "One man on a mission," he said softly, walking to his rental. He'd picked up a nondescript midsize Chevy SUV this time. He had no particular preference in rental cars, although he liked comfort. He was rather attached to several of the cars in his garage back in Carmel. His custom restored 1971 Ford F-150 pickup was a favorite, but didn't have the history of the 1982 Trans Am that had been one of the K.I.T.T. cars on *Knight Rider,* his boyhood favorite television series. He also loved his new red Cadillac CTS and the custom black Land Rover that had just been delivered. His two motorcycles also occupied space in the large garage, which was built into the hillside of his property.

After checking in, he unpacked, removed his bandit clothes and took a quick shower. Later, he watched the end of the *Sunday Night Football* game stretched out on the king-size bed, warm and comfy in sweats. He must have dozed off, because suddenly he jerked awake, certain he'd heard something. Was that the pinging of pebbles on his window?

Wyatt swung his legs off the bed and immediately felt the aftereffects of his unaccustomed horseback-riding adventure. He'd used muscles in ways that the Nautilus machine in his home gym and the rock wall built into the exterior of his house just couldn't duplicate. Hobbling to the window, he looked out into the black night. He didn't see a thing. He listened, but heard nothing else. He went outside, noticing that the wind had picked up from the northwest and the temperature had dropped.

Toni was not in the bushes, trying to get his attention. He must have imagined that she'd come back to the motel, looking for him.

He shivered in the cold night air, then went back inside his room. Tomorrow, he'd begin the courtship of Miss Mayor.

He still balked at the idea of getting married, but he couldn't deny that he wanted to be with Toni now. Could she take a chance that he might someday want forever? He didn't know. He knew it was a big gamble.

He'd opened himself to Toni as he'd never done with another person. Which only made sense, since she'd been his best friend, his first lover and the woman he could never forget.

DESPITE TONI'S DOUBTS about Wyatt's staged abduction, she had to admit the result had been positive. More people than she'd ever expected had come to her office. They'd asked her if she'd known about the stagecoach, if the bandit had indeed surprised her, if a stagecoach was as romantic as a carriage ride. Then they'd nibbled on her food, looked at the architect's renderings of the hotel project and asked when they could see the inside. Was she going to have a model condo? When would the retail space be ready?

And then Clarissa, Venetia, Bobbi Jean and Ida came in and asked if she and Wyatt were back together again, if he was staying in town and what was up next for them. Toni swore she had nothing planned, doubted that Wyatt did and that she was sure he'd be headed back to California soon. The ladies did not appear to believe her, which was slightly depressing.

If she only focused on her business and her political career, she was happy. If she had to answer personal questions, she'd soon panic.

Whenever she thought about Wyatt's ability to steal her heart, she felt like running out of her office. Out of town. Out of the state. She hadn't begun to get over his initial reappearance in her life, and now he was back. How could she gather her defenses when her emotions were such a jumble?

She needed a strong drink—of Earl Grey tea, preferably.

"What's wrong?" Christie asked as she joined Toni in the small kitchenette area and closed the door behind her.

"Wyatt," Toni answered, dunking her tea bag vigorously in the hot water. "He was the bandit, of course."

"I suspected as much. So, was it romantic?"

"No. Being abducted from a public holiday event is embarrassing."

"But exciting, right?"

"No! I mean, a little bit, but the point is I don't want to be excited. I want to be…competent. Productive. I want to inspire faith in the people of Brody's Crossing, not make them snicker about whether the bandit kissed me or not!"

"Well, did he?" Christie asked with a grin.

"Oh! I just want things to go back to normal."

"Do you? What if Wyatt really cares about you?"

"He's a billionaire adventurer and a confirmed bachelor. Despite admitting that he returned to town to pursue a relationship with me, I don't believe he'll stay."

"Why?"

"Because I don't believe he's really changed all that much. I mean, he's more mature than he was at eighteen and he understands himself better now, but he's not the type of man who can be happy in a small town with a woman who has to care a lot about her public image."

"I got the impression everyone liked Wyatt."

"He's very likable. He's charming and he can do things for people, for the town, like no one else."

"Why are you so sure he won't stay?"

Toni looked down, feeling overwhelmed again. How could she explain this to Christie, who hadn't grown up with them? She hadn't cried with Toni when she'd been jilted by the boyfriend she'd thought she would spend the rest of her life with. "He left me before, Christie, right after graduation. One day we were a couple. The next day he was headed to Stanford, never to look back." She sniffled, then continued. "That's the way Wyatt is. Always looking forward. Always ready for the next adventure."

Christie put her arm around Toni's shoulders. "Maybe you're his next big adventure."

"I don't think so. I don't even think I want to be."

"Aren't you curious? What if the two of you are meant to be together?"

"This isn't a movie, Christie. This is my life. He can't just pop in and think I'm going to change my goals, my responsibilities."

"Isn't there any room in your life for him?"

"I don't think you understand Wyatt—at least the Wyatt I know. You don't make room for him. *He* makes room for *you*."

Chapter Twelve

On Monday morning Wyatt got up early, went for a run around the downtown area and then jogged by the old hotel site, where workers were unloading their trucks and making a general racket. He didn't see Toni's pickup—of which he had very fond memories—so he continued around the corner on Commerce Street to the café.

Thanks to the cool temperatures, he wasn't too sweaty to go inside and have breakfast. He hadn't shaved, so he was a bit rough-looking, but surely the morning crowd wouldn't mind. He'd appeared in public in far worse situations in the past, including wearing only a loincloth and nothing at all.

"Hey there, Wyatt."

"Good morning, Claude."

"That was some stunt last night. Real entertaining."

"Glad you enjoyed it." He walked a little farther before being stopped again.

"Wyatt," Chief Montoya said with a nod. "I had my doubts about that stagecoach when you called me, but it turned out okay."

"The driver is a real professional."

"Well, it turned out to be a good addition to the Settlers' Stroll. You certainly have livened up the Christmas festivities this year."

Wyatt chuckled. "I do my best."

He made his way to an empty booth. He was rather amazed that everyone treated him as just another citizen of the town, as if he hadn't been gone for fifteen years. They seemed to accept that all those years ago he'd been a kid, acting out and getting into mischief, and now he was an adult.

He felt remarkably well despite getting little encouragement from Toni the other night. She'd only promised to think about their relationship. She hadn't called him or come by the motel, but that was okay. He needed to give her time.

He wondered if a week was enough. After all, they'd known each other practically their whole lives. Well, they didn't know much about each other over the past fifteen years, but each of them had known where the other was and basically what they were doing. That counted, right?

He stopped his mental discussions to order an old-fashioned breakfast of ham and eggs, crispy hash browns, toast and coffee. Normally he had fruit and yogurt for breakfast—his daily stab at nutritious eating, in case the rest of the day consisted of snacks and business lunches. The waitress filled his coffee mug and left.

"Hey, Wyatt. I thought that was you on the horse last night," James said less than a minute later, swinging into the booth. "What's up?"

"Back in town for a little holiday R & R," Wyatt answered. "Why aren't you having breakfast with your lovely bride?"

"She left early this morning for a Christmas shopping trip with Clarissa, Christie and Ida. They're headed to Fort Worth for the day. Closed the salon and everything."

"Sounds like that could be a long day."

"Maybe, and an expensive one. So, are you here alone?"

"Yes. I didn't need publicity or assistance doing anything, so I just hopped on a flight and came to visit my hometown during the holiday."

"And see Toni," James added before motioning to the waitress for coffee.

Wyatt smiled and shrugged. "What can I say? It was good seeing her again. I… Maybe I shouldn't have stayed away so long."

"Perhaps you both needed time." James got his coffee and ordered a waffle and bacon.

"I don't know where we stand," Wyatt admitted when the waitress left. "We're kind of feeling our way through this."

"Yeah, I can see that. Abducting her in a stagecoach. Very subtle and touchy-feely." James laughed.

"Hey, I thought it was creative and kind of romantic."

"You always did have a knack for over-the-top spectacles."

Wyatt frowned. "Do you think it was too over-the-top?"

James sighed. "Wyatt, you have to think about Toni. It's not what you're doing, it's how she sees it."

"I guess you're right."

"Believe me, I know a little more about women now that I'm married. Sandy was as skittish as a yearling when she first stopped in town, just passing through on her way to California. Her car broke down and she worked for Clarissa for a few weeks. When we started, er, seeing each other, she was more concerned about my reputation than I was. She didn't want anyone to know that she'd been to my apartment or that we were dating, since she thought she was too wild for me and she was leaving town. And then there was that big dustup at the courthouse in Graham, where she marched right up with about fifty of her closest friends to defend me publicly."

"I saw the photos from the newspaper online. That was some sight. What did they call themselves, redheaded floozies?"

"That's right, taken from something another attorney said about Sandy, who went by Scarlett back then. But the point is that women are sensitive about things like reputations and public opinion."

"I know, and Toni is especially so because she's mayor."

"Exactly. You have to consider that."

Wyatt shifted uncomfortably in his seat. "I know, and I try. But then I get an idea or she does something, and I act before I think."

"If you're going to impress her, you've got to think of her first. What would she like? How would she see your efforts?"

"You're right. So, any ideas on what women like?"

"Every one is different, man. That's what makes life interesting."

Conversation stopped as the waitress brought their food, refilled their coffee and left their checks.

"Toni used to like movies. We would go to the Rialto and sit in the balcony, and once we drove all the way to Granbury to go to the drive-in. That was fun. Her parents were out of town and she was supposed to be staying with Jennifer, but—"

"Hey, sounds like most of the movie-going was about you making out with Toni. What about the *movies?*"

Wyatt sighed. "You're right. This relationship thing is harder than it looks," he grumbled as he cut his ham.

"But very worthwhile in the end."

"Only if it turns out right."

"Then make sure it turns out right."

Easier said than done, Wyatt thought as he poked at his eggs, his appetite waning. Was he up to an old-fashioned courtship, or would he resort to something fun if times got tough? He really didn't know. His personal demons had cheated her out of the engagement and wedding she'd expected fifteen years ago. He owed it to himself, and especially to Toni, to try to put his past to rest once and for all.

Toni worked at the hotel job site in the morning, before heading to her office. She had some subcontractors to coordinate with, then some final work on the budget. The last city council meeting was tonight, a private session to tweak the final product. They'd present it to the public in January.

Then, Toni had to decide if she was running for mayor again.

She really didn't know what she would do. She loved this town and they'd made such progress in the past three years. New businesses, renovations and new people moving in. But she knew it wasn't only because she was the mayor. Lots of factors played into the mix.

If she wasn't mayor, she'd still be part of the renewal of Brody's Crossing. She'd be doing the actual work in many cases.

Plus, she might have a chance at a personal life.

There was no guarantee, though. What if she didn't run for reelection, and then she never got that perfect-ever-after ending that she wanted? Would she feel as if she'd failed?

She put her head between her hands. She felt so much pressure from all angles. Job deadlines, political decisions, personal dilemmas, and to top it all off, Wyatt McCall.

He wanted a chance at a relationship. The problem was that she'd given him a chance fifteen years ago and he'd broken her heart. Why should she believe that they could make a go of a serious relationship now, when they were even more different?

She heard the door open and straightened up, pushing her hair back, patting her eyes and putting a pleasant expression on her face. Perhaps this was a new client. But, no, she realized when she saw the reflection in the hall mirror. With his usual impeccable timing for finding her weak moments, Wyatt had just strolled into the office, dressed in tailored jeans and a cable-knit fisherman's sweater, his leather jacket and brown boots.

As usual, he took her breath away. And just as usual, she struggled for a snappy remark to keep him at arm's length.

"Is your horse double-parked outside?"

"No, he had to go back to Weatherford. Our brief but memorable time together is over."

"No doubt the story of many of your nights."

"Hah! You've been reading too many gossip columns."

"Not really," she said in what she hoped was a haughty tone. "Your other fans in town do talk, though."

He came over and rested one hip on her desk. "Aren't you a fan? I know for sure I'm a big fan of yours."

Her heart sped up as she resisted the urge to roll her desk chair backward. That would be juvenile, and probably make Wyatt laugh. "Thanks, but I don't believe in fan clubs."

"Do you believe in dating? Because I'd like to ask you out."

"On a date?"

"What did I just say?" he answered with a smile. "Yes, real date. As in dinner and a movie."

"When?"

He shrugged. "Tonight. Tomorrow night. Whatever works with your schedule."

"I have a closed-door city council meeting tonight on the budget," she blurted out.

"That's okay. How about tomorrow?"

"No."

"Nothing scheduled, or no date?"

"No, I don't have anything scheduled, but—"

"Great! Can I pick you up at your house, or do we need to meet somewhere?"

She felt a moment of panic, which logically she shouldn't feel since it was perfectly acceptable for her to go out on a date. It would be suspicious for her to sneak around in the middle of the night, as she had last Sunday. But Wyatt was talking about ringing her doorbell, taking her out in his vehicle and bringing her home at a reasonable hour. A date. She could do this.

"You can pick me up," she finally said. "However, I have to be at the job site early on Wednesday, so I can't make it a late night."

"How about if I check the schedule for movies? There

should be something on around seven or eight. That should get you back by ten or so. Is that okay?"

"Yes, that would be great." And why was Wyatt being so reasonable and sensible? That wasn't like him at all. Of course, he had said he wanted a chance, and maybe this was his way of turning over a new leaf.

"Good. Maybe I'll see you around before then."

"Um, maybe."

"Bye, then," he said, and leaned forward and kissed her lightly. He smelled so good and looked so enticing that she was tempted to grab his jacket and pull him closer. Deepen the kiss. Ask him to stay.

But, no, she couldn't. She shouldn't. She wouldn't.

"Bye," she said weakly as he pulled back and smiled. "See you tomorrow."

WYATT RESISTED THE URGE to plan something spectacular. The problem with having lots of money, he realized, was that you could do things in such a big way that you overwhelmed people. He could, for example, build a pavilion, hire a chef and an orchestra and plan anything else he wanted for a special date. He could fly in a movie and have it projected on a custom-built screen. He could, but he shouldn't, so he settled on calling Dewey's to make sure he could get a good table for Tuesday night.

There were two movies playing at the Rialto, and one of them was strictly for children. He was not taking Toni on their first real date in fifteen years to see talking cartoon characters. The other was a sappy romantic chick flick, which he supposed she'd like and he could sit through, although he might need a testosterone booster afterward.

He called Toni and immediately got her voice mail. He'd rather talk to her in person, but he left a message. "Hey, ba— I mean, Toni. I checked the schedule and the movie is at seven-thirty. I'll pick you up at six o'clock. This time, I'll be driving a white SUV. No stagecoach. See you then. Bye."

It was odd, he thought as he sat in his rental car outside the theater, that talking to Toni, going on a date with her, even antagonizing her, seemed so normal. As if fifteen years hadn't passed and they weren't such different people now.

Hell, maybe they weren't. Maybe people really didn't change all that much. When he'd come back to Brody's Crossing before, however, he hadn't felt as if he could slip back in so easily. Now, he did. Had he changed, or was it the circumstances?

He didn't know. If he'd still been seeing a therapist, as he had many years ago, he might have called up and asked. But this was one of those times in life where you just had to go with the flow. Find out what felt right and hope you made the right choices.

His instincts said the way to Toni's heart was to take their relationship slow and easy. Not his strong suit, but he was trying. One date at a time. That's the way they'd get to…what? He wasn't sure. The idea of marriage still scared him, but not having Toni in his life maybe scared him more.

He started the engine, then glanced at the clock. He had several hours before he needed to get ready for his date. Maybe he'd get Toni some flowers. The only place he knew of was Casale's Grocery, which meant possibly running into her mother or father. At the least, she might recognize the type of arrangement or the wrapping. Better to drive to Graham and get some there. She'd know he'd made more of an effort. If he remembered dating correctly, women liked to know the man had gone out of his way to try to make them happy.

Just not too much. Not overboard, as was his usual inclination. No pavilions, orchestras or private chefs. No orchids flown in from Japan. Just a regular date.

Sometimes, being "normal" was harder than planning something spectacular.

ON TUESDAY TONI TOOK OFF early to get ready for her date. She couldn't recall when her last date had occurred, although she remembered that the man had been a farm-implements salesman she'd met at a Chamber of Commerce meeting in Graham. The night had been awkward at best, and had resulted in no subsequent dates.

Toni figured she was so rusty in the dating department that she'd never have another one. At least, not around here.

And yet, here she was, standing in front of her closet, still damp from her shower, experiencing major angst over what she was going to wear. Jeans and a nice sweater, or long skirt and boots, or what? She had a few pantsuits she wore to public events, but those were too conservative and formal for a date with Wyatt. Jeans seemed so casual and ordinary. She moved through the hangers, frowning at her choices. She needed to go shopping if she was going out on dates.

Wyatt had mentioned he liked her legs. Should she show them off? Darn it, it was cold outside tonight! She couldn't wear a short skirt and nothing on her legs. Then she remembered some tights she'd bought. She could wear a pullover sweater, short denim skirt and tights. She moved more hangers aside.

Or she could be daring and wear this red zip-front sweater, she thought, holding it up. That would probably drive Wyatt crazy. If he made any remarks, she could simply say it was red, for Christmas. Plus, they'd be in public, not off making out as they had done so many nights when they were teenagers.

Tonight, she was not going to sit in the balcony, nor was she going to let Wyatt pull down her zipper. Even if he sweet-talked her and told her how pretty she was.

Just in case, though, she was going to wear her new red lace Miracle Bra. As her mother always reminded her, wear nice underwear on the off chance you have to go to the emergency room. As she decided on her clothing for tonight, she felt so

young again. How many times had she called her best friend
to ask what she was wearing on their double dates? Coordi-
nating clothes was important, so that one person didn't over-
or under-dress. Plus, you wouldn't want to end up both
wearing the same thing.

She had the strongest urge to call Jennifer, to laugh with
her about how they'd gone on dates together and all the fun
things they'd done. She glanced at the clock. Jennifer was
probably fixing supper for her family or helping Hailey with
her homework. Jennifer probably didn't have time to talk to
an old friend just now. When Toni had tried to call before,
Jennifer had always seemed too busy to chat.

The estrangement from her former best friend made Toni
sad. She didn't know how to blend their lives together. Maybe
if they had something in common... But they didn't. Not
right now, anyway. Someday, if Toni married and had a family,
then maybe they would be able to relate better.

With a sigh, she took the red sweater, bra, skirt and tights
into the bathroom. She had just enough time to get ready
for her date.

"WHAT DID YOU DO TODAY?" Toni asked Wyatt as they drove
west on Elm Street, toward Dewey's Steak House and Saloon.
They were running a little late because she'd taken the beautiful flowers he'd brought her inside and put them in a vase.
She especially liked them because they weren't from her
family's grocery store.

"Nothing illegal or very exciting," he answered. "I went
Christmas shopping."

"Really? Where did you go?"

"Looking for hints as to what you might get?"

"No!" As a matter of fact, she'd never thought about getting
a Christmas gift from Wyatt. She hadn't expected him to be
here for the holiday. Now she had to get him a gift and include

him in their celebrations! "Really, don't feel obligated to get me anything."

"I don't. I just like to find things that people might like. I haven't found the perfect something for you, but I did find a terrific gift for the Brodys."

"Oh?"

"Mr. and Mrs. Brody are getting too old to ride their property on horseback, especially since he had a stroke. And James and Sandy are out there often, so I got them four all-terrain vehicles. ATVs, a lot like I had when we were younger."

"I thought those were mostly for kids and hunters."

"No, they're for everyone. The salesman at the dealership told me lots of ranchers use them. I think James and his father, especially, will get a kick out of them."

"Yes, I'm sure they will."

"Have you ridden an ATV since you graduated from high school?"

"No, of course not. Why would I? Where would I?"

"I'll see if James will let us use his, as soon as they're delivered."

"Well, I'll see."

"Come on, where's your sense of adventure?"

"Firmly locked in a box on a top shelf in my closet, where I can keep it away from the reality of broken bones. The older I get, the more concerned I am about my mortality."

Wyatt laughed and turned right on the road to Dewey's. The sun had set and the night was dark. Toni thought of another night, when she'd driven him with stealth to the water tower. She felt a little strange to be out in public with Wyatt, partly as if they were both eighteen again, and partly as if they were near-strangers who hadn't made love—correction, had sex— beneath the stars just ten days ago.

There had been no talk of love as they'd lost themselves

in each other. There had been little talking at all until later, when Wyatt had become amazingly chatty.

Tonight, they shared a surprisingly fun dinner of salads, steaks, baked potatoes and a glass of red wine each. Nothing extravagant. They saw a lot of people they both knew, but no one seemed all that surprised to see them out in public together. Toni looked around for anyone who seemed to be whispering about them, but she didn't see anyone.

Okay. So far, so good. She breathed a sigh of relief when Wyatt paid the tab and left a generous tip. He helped her into her leather jacket like a perfect gentleman and escorted her outside.

"You know that sweater is driving me crazy, don't you?" he said when they settled in the SUV for the drive to the theater.

"Really? It's red. For Christmas."

"It has a zipper. For unzipping."

"It's a fashion statement."

"It's a temptation."

She wouldn't dare let him know she was secretly pleased. Payback was tough, she thought. "You're not going to do anything about it, though, right? You promised to be on your best behavior."

"Don't you remember that old saying. 'When she was good, she was very, very good. And when she was bad, she was terrific.' That applies to men, as well."

"Hmm."

"You were terrific last weekend, you know."

She kept her expression bland. Bored, really. But inside she smiled. "We're starting over, remember? Last weekend didn't exist."

"Oh, yeah, it did. But I'm willing to avoid talking about it, if that makes you happy."

"I'm just looking forward to the movie."

Wyatt ran his gaze up and down the zipper on her sweater. "Me, too."

The Rialto wasn't crowded on a Tuesday night. They'd strung bright white lights around the marquee and poster windows. Inside, a silver tree stood beside the end of the concession stand. The interior of the theater hadn't been changed in twenty or thirty years, and Toni really felt as if she and Wyatt were reliving the past.

"Come here," he said, taking her hand and pulling her toward the balcony.

"I'm not sitting up there with you. No way."

"Okay, but just let me go upstairs and see the old place. I have a lot of good memories of that balcony."

"We are not making out in the balcony."

"As much as I enjoyed that, there are other memories, too," he said, pulling her toward the staircase. A thick red velvet rope with a clip on one end barred their entrance, but Wyatt made quick work of that obstacle.

"Wyatt, we're going to get into trouble," Toni whispered.

"No, I already asked the manager if I could just go upstairs to see the old place. He said it was okay."

"I'm not sure I believe you."

"Why would I lie about something so simple?" he asked, sounding genuinely confused. "You could always ask him."

She rolled her eyes. "Oh, okay, then. Go on." She shook her head at his grin and tromped up the stairs after him. She was not going first, where he could stare at her bottom.

In the musty, dimly lit balcony, time had indeed stood still. The old projector, just over their heads, sent a stream of dusty light toward the screen, on which a cartoon trash can was gobbling up empty cups and candy wrappers. The smell of old velvet fabric, spilled soft drinks and popcorn permeated the air.

"This place is still exactly like it was when we were kids," she said.

"Yeah, isn't that great? I used to shoot my water gun down

to the front row, hitting you and Jennifer, if you were in the audience, or any of my other classmates or friends."

"I remember that. You threw popcorn, too."

"No, that was James. He didn't have a water gun."

"Good thing. One was enough." Toni folded her jacket over her arm and wandered down the row. On the screen below, the previews were starting. She felt Wyatt more than heard him over the soundtrack.

"We should find a seat down there," she whispered, turning back so he could hear her.

"You always did like the previews."

She nodded, letting herself feel the past. The memory of another movie date pushed into her thoughts. She and Wyatt, Jennifer and Tommy, double-dating, sitting in the balcony. They'd gone to see *A Few Good Men,* although she and Jennifer had wanted to see *The Last of the Mohicans* again. They could have sat through that movie a hundred times, staring at Daniel Day-Lewis running through the forest with his long rifle. Yummy.

And since they'd seen *A Few Good Men* before and Wyatt and Tommy already knew most of the dialogue, she and Wyatt had ended up pairing off and making out. She'd worn a blouse with cute little tabs instead of buttonholes. Wyatt had managed to get them open, but when the manager stomped up the steps in the middle of the movie, neither she nor Wyatt had been able to get them closed. She'd been terribly embarrassed, certain that she'd be sent home in disgrace, her white lace demicup bra showing. Instead, the boys had been sent downstairs and she and Jennifer had sat upstairs, silently watching a movie they didn't want to see.

"Toni?" Wyatt said, bringing her back to the present.

"Yes?" she managed to say before he kissed her.

Chapter Thirteen

Wyatt's kiss was sweet, his lips soft and firm. Her folded jacket kept them from coming together fully, which was just as well because she was tempted to put her arms around him and keep him in this balcony for as long as the movie was playing. But that would defeat the purpose of dating, spending time in public and seeing if they had a future together rather than just a past.

He pulled back. "If you're going to keep me away from that zipper, we should really go downstairs."

"You're right. Enough of the walk down memory lane."

"I have some very good memories of this place."

"I have good and bad. I don't think you ever realized how much I dreaded getting caught doing something we shouldn't have been doing. That time we were discovered with my blouse unbuttoned was particularly embarrassing."

"I'm sorry. Most of the time it seemed funny to me."

"You never got into any trouble."

"That's not exactly true, but I didn't get into trouble like the rest of you."

"I don't want to feel that way again, like I'm doing something wrong and everyone will know."

"And judge you."

"Well, yes. They'll have their opinion, and let's face it. If

I get caught undressed in public as an adult, as their mayor, they have a right to be judgmental. And even angry. They put their faith in me and I let them down."

"Still, you're not a nun. Or a saint."

"No, but I'm supposed to be a good example. That means I have to be careful."

"I'm not going to do anything to compromise your reputation."

"I want to believe you, Wyatt. Really, I do."

He sighed. "I know it's going to take more than words."

"You're doing fine." She felt as if she should cross her fingers or knock on wood. How long could Wyatt remain "good"?

"Sometimes, I wish you weren't the mayor."

She didn't know what to say to that, so she took his hand and led him down the stairs. The movie was starting and this conversation had come to an end.

WYATT HAD HOPED TONI would ask him to come into her house when he took her home. She reminded him that she had an early morning at the job site on Wednesday, so she couldn't stay up late. Then she'd leaned across the console and kissed him until his toes curled. When she pulled back, she said that he was so tempting that she couldn't trust herself alone with him, and then she'd smiled sweetly and gotten out of the SUV. He'd scrambled to catch up, walk her to her door and act like a gentleman.

How was a man supposed to react when a woman said he was too tempting? She'd told him that twice now. He wanted to push her door open, pick her up in his arms and carry her into her bedroom, à la Clark Gable in *Gone with the Wind*.

But Rhett Butler was *married* to Scarlett O'Hara in that classic movie, plus he was trying to prove something. Wyatt wasn't married, and he was still having a hard time contemplating taking such a big step. Even with a woman he'd known most of his life and wanted so much he could barely see straight.

He was too wound up to go back to the motel, so he drove out to Dewey's to have a beer and listen to some bar talk.

Unfortunately, there were only five guys listening to country-western music, watching a Stars game and sipping brews. Three of them were cowboys he didn't know. One was Bud Hammer, who'd been a grumpy old man years ago, and the last one was Leo Casale.

He wasn't sure how he felt about chatting with Toni's brother, but it was too late now. Wyatt knew he'd been spotted.

"Hey, Leo," he said, taking the bar stool between him and Bud. "What's up?"

"My cable's out," he replied, "so I came here to watch the game."

"You should sue that cable company," Bud advised.

Leo shook his head and ignored the older man. "What's up with you? Didn't you have a date with my sister tonight?"

"I did, and I got her home nice and early, as requested."

Leo looked surprised. "Good for you. She'll like that."

"It's the least I could do. She has a lot going on in her life."

"Woman mayor," Wyatt heard Bud grumble. "Doesn't seem right." The curmudgeon slapped a few dollars on the bar and walked off.

Leo took a sip of beer, then said, "Yes, she does. The hotel project is a big one. We've got our own money and time invested in this one, along with Christie Crawford's bankroll. Toni's also been working hard on the Christmas activities and the budget."

"She said her final city council meeting was last night."

"It was, but she'll probably still have more to do. There's always something going on." Leo took a drink from his longneck, then glanced at Wyatt. "Are you up for that? The demands of her office? She loves her job as mayor and her career as a renovator, you know."

Wyatt felt like twisting on his bar stool. Had Leo been

reading his mind? "I have to admit, I think Toni works too hard sometimes. I think she should spend more time having fun. But, if being mayor is what makes her happy, then that's something I can live with."

"Sounds like you're planning a long-term relationship."

"It's a scary idea for me, but your sister is special."

"Special enough to marry?"

Wasn't that the real question? "She's definitely special enough to marry. Whether I'm the right man for her is another question. And truthfully, I don't know the answer to that one."

"Well, that's honest." Leo took a sip of beer. "Just don't mess with her head. She got on with her life after college, but she never really got over you, you know."

"I guess I knew that on some level, but I hadn't thought about it much until recently." Guilt, most likely, had driven the memories away. That, and the fact that Wyatt didn't spend much time in town and had gone out of his way to avoid Toni, Leo and their parents in the past.

"She doesn't date. She's never had a serious boyfriend since you left town. Did you know that?"

"No, I didn't." Toni was so beautiful and talented. Any man would be lucky to spend time with her. And she was a young, healthy woman, who obviously enjoyed going out and having fun. Having sex. He shifted uncomfortably on the seat. The idea of Toni with another man was more than upsetting, which was another sign that he was headed toward something more serious than he'd have thought possible just two weeks ago.

"I was barely a teenager when you left her before, so I didn't understand everything that was going on. But I'm a man now, Wyatt." Leo sat his empty beer bottle down on the bar with a decided thunk. "Don't mess with her head again."

Wyatt filled in the blank. *Or else.* He believed Leo was serious. Wyatt just needed to figure out how serious he was about a relationship with Toni, because the more time he spent with her and the longer he stayed in Brody's Crossing, the more he realized it was going to be all or nothing.

TONI AND LEO MET WITH their flooring subcontractor early Wednesday morning. For simple hardwood, tile or laminate floors, she had her own crews do the installation. However, Christie had suggested vintage-style black-and-white marble pattern for the foyer, reclaimed oak planks for the restaurant and bar areas and granite tiles for the restrooms. Toni had initially hesitated about the cost and inconvenience of laying so many different floors, but then she'd begun to appreciate Christie's vision of the place and she knew they had to go forward.

After the flooring contractor had finished taking measurements and conducting an examination of the subfloor, he left with a promise to send an estimate later in the day. Christie checked on the progress of the wainscoting and drywall, then left for breakfast at the café with an informal group of business owners. They were excited about the opening of the hotel project and wanted to discuss the possibility of renovating the old train station. Toni didn't think that the train station project was viable at this time, but she would listen to their objectives. Perhaps there was something the city could do, although the money wasn't in the budget this next year.

Her busy morning left her little time to think about her date. Her very normal, very "nice" date. Wyatt had been a gentleman, with just a brief kiss during their balcony detour. She'd been apprehensive most of the night, afraid that he'd do something wild to live up to his reputation. But he'd behaved himself, just as he'd promised.

At the end of the evening she'd been almost disappointed, which was an odd reaction. She thought she wanted Wyatt to behave himself, but when he did, he didn't seem quite like himself.

She shook her head to clear her thoughts as she parked in

back of her office. She had some calls to make, and then later Sandy was going to trim her hair at Clarissa's House of Style. Toni decided she might even splurge on a manicure. Just for herself. Not because she was dating one of the world's most eligible bachelors.

She would push Wyatt out of her mind until he got in touch with her again. He'd promised to call later. Until then, she was focusing on her business.

"No, I'll call her," Wyatt promised his mother. "We'll see you around six o'clock."

His mother wanted him to bring Toni to dinner at their house tonight. For what reason, he didn't have a clue. He probably should have spent another evening with his parents already, but he'd been busy. He'd gone all the way to Dallas for some Christmas shopping, and he'd spent time in front of his laptop on an online conference call regarding the foundation.

Besides, he didn't see the point of too much parental socializing. They rarely had anything to talk about except the weather, their friends—many of whom he didn't know or could no longer remember—and upcoming vacations.

Sometimes he wished he had a closer relationship with both his mother and father, but that probably wasn't going to happen at this late date. They just didn't have much in common, and he still had a lot of resentment. Plus, his mother harbored her own guilt over her drinking all through his childhood and teenage years. She hadn't gotten sober until he was in college, and only then because of a medical crisis.

Stop drinking or die, the doctor had told her. She'd stopped. Not because of her family, but for herself.

So if she wanted Toni to come to dinner tonight, there was a selfish reason, Wyatt was sure.

On the other hand, he now had a reason to call Toni that

didn't seem made up. Before his mother's call, he'd been trying to think of some ordinary reason to see Toni tonight.

He could still think of lots of extraordinary things they could do together. Fly to Europe, watch the sun set in Carmel, see a Broadway play in New York City. He was coming up short on what he could do that was reasonable from Toni's standpoint, plus fit her schedule. He couldn't ask her to fly off with him on a whim, when she had civic obligations and a major renovation project going on. The holidays hadn't meant all that much to him, other than extra parties and reasons to buy expensive gifts. But to Toni and most of the people of Brody's Crossing, Christmas was about traditions, friendships and good food.

The solution was inside him. He just had to get back to his own roots in this community.

TONI GOT TO THE SALON a few minutes early and found that Jennifer was still sitting in Sandy's chair, her cell phone pressed to her ear.

"No, no, I understand," she said to the person on the other end. "Just get better and I'll call you next time." She pressed a button, folded up her cell phone and looked so despondent that Toni had to speak.

"Jennifer. Is everything okay?"

Her former best friend looked up with big blue eyes. "Oh, it's not so bad. Not like Hailey having a problem." She sniffed a little, then sighed. "It's just that…she has a program tonight at church. The first one she could participate in since her treatments ended last year. And Tommy Jr. has a terrible sore throat and cough, so we got a babysitter. Now the babysitter is sick, and Tommy and I can't both go to Hailey's program because almost everyone else we know is already going or is sitting for someone else."

"I'm so sorry." Seeing their daughter back to her old self

was such a joy for Jennifer and Tommy, Toni knew. Hailey had finished chemo last year and now she looked the picture of health. "Could I babysit for Tommy Jr.?"

"You?"

"Well, yes. I know I don't have any children, but I like them and they seem to like me. And I know first aid and I have common sense. Plus, if anything came up, I could call you or my mother for advice."

"No, it's not that I don't trust you. It's just that you're...well, you're the mayor. And a businesswoman. And you're dating Wyatt McCall! Why would you want to spend a night babysitting Tommy Jr. when you could be out with him?"

"Oh, please. You were my best friend. I know we're not as close as we once were—" *or as I'd like to be,* Toni silently added "—but that doesn't mean I stopped caring about you and your family."

"It just never occurred to me that you'd want to do something so...ordinary."

Toni laughed, since the remark struck her as so silly. "What, you think I have a glamorous life because I have my own business? I tear out things and build things, for heaven's sake! Usually I have calluses and splinters, plus a few bruises and a scratch or two. And as for the mayor part, well, that's a working job, too. Most of the time I read reports and sit in meetings. Again, hardly glamorous."

"I suppose. I just never thought about it like that."

"Well, now you know," Toni replied, putting her hand on Jennifer's arm. "I'd love to spend the evening babysitting Tommy Jr. so you and Tommy can attend Hailey's program at church."

Jennifer still looked so much like the best friend Toni had known almost all her life that she reached out and hugged her. "Thank you," Jennifer said, the words muffled against Toni's jacket. "I really want to go to the church tonight."

"I understand. What time do I need to be there?"

"About six-thirty."

"Okay."

"Toni?"

"What?"

"If Wyatt comes to see you at my house, no hanky-panky, okay?" Jennifer said this so deadpan that Toni felt floored.

Then her friend smiled and giggled. And they laughed together, hugging, thinking back on all the times they'd snuck their boyfriends in when they were supposed to be alone or babysitting or studying. Tommy and Wyatt, the boys they'd loved.

Tommy, the boy Jennifer had married right out of high school. How their lives had changed.

Toni pulled back, still smiling. "After the holidays, maybe we can get together. I have some things to tell you."

"Okay. That's a girl date." Jennifer hopped down from Sandy's chair and reached for her coat. "I'll see you tonight at six-thirty. Do you know which house is ours?"

"Sure, I remember." She'd been there five years ago for a high-school reunion kickoff party, but she'd felt so out of place. Most of their classmates had families. Lots of photos had been passed around.

Toni didn't even have a pet she could show off in pictures. How sad was that? She'd devoted all her time to her business, and shortly after the party had decided to run for mayor.

They hugged once more, then Toni removed her jacket and sat in her chair. Sandy moved closer and adjusted the lift.

"That was so sweet. If I'd known she needed a babysitter, I would have volunteered. Hailey was a customer the first week I worked here."

"They're a lucky family." Hailey had survived her medical crisis, and Tommy and Jennifer seemed just as much in love as they had when they were eighteen.

"Yes, they are. Lucky to have a friend like you."

Toni looked down. Maybe it wasn't too late to be a best friend again. Maybe she should have tried a little harder before this.

"So, what are we doing today?" Sandy asked, fluffing Toni's hair.

ON THE WALK BACK TO HER OFFICE, Toni's cell phone rang. She looked at the caller ID. Wyatt. Her heart began to race as she walked quickly up Main Street toward her office. She pressed the button to answer the call.

"Hello, Wyatt."

"You look really good. Is that a new haircut?"

She looked around, almost giving herself whiplash. "Where are you?" She didn't see the white SUV anywhere.

He stepped out onto the sidewalk from the shadowed overhang of the Burger Barn. "Gotcha."

"Are you spying on me?" she asked into the phone, even as she looked both ways to cross the street and join him.

"No, I was having a late lunch." He disconnected the call and slipped his cell phone into his pocket, a grin on his face.

She flipped her own phone closed and put it in her jacket. She couldn't keep herself from smiling, either, even though she was in the middle of town and probably looked like a lovesick teenager.

Lovesick? No, she was not going to fall for Wyatt again so soon, before she knew what his intentions were. Been there, done that, and it hurt too much.

"Hey, you looked so glad to see me, but now you're frowning. What's up?"

She shook off her thoughts. "Nothing. I am glad to see you," she said, smiling again. "Do you really like my hair?"

"It's very bouncy," he said, fingering the ends, which were still long but had a bit more shape than before.

"My hair is always bouncy when Sandy finishes with me. Then when I fix it, it's mostly flat again. I don't have her skill."

"Yeah, but I bet she can't use a nail gun like you can."

Toni laughed. "That's true."

"Are you going back to your office?"

"Yes."

"I'll walk with you. I parked the SUV up there."

"Did you come there to see me?"

"Yes, but I saw your Out to Lunch sign and decided to treat myself to a burger."

"The quality of meat has gone up since the new butcher shop opened."

"And I noticed they have bison burgers on the menu. Interesting."

"And tasty. They come from the Crawford ranch. The Rocking C."

"I thought they only raised Herefords."

"Up until a few years ago. When Cal went to Afghanistan for active military service, Troy came in to run the ranch and found it was in financial trouble. He ended up selling off most of the Herefords, bringing in bison and subleasing the land for organic dairy cows and free-range chickens."

"Wow. That is a huge transformation."

"Lots of things have changed around here, Wyatt."

"Not you. You're as pretty as ever."

"And you're as full of it as ever. I'm fifteen years older and I know it."

"You're prettier than ever. And now you're more accomplished. That's something no one can say when they're eighteen."

"True. I don't want to go back—I'm just pointing out that we're all different."

"Point taken. Now, for today's burning question. Will you have dinner with me tonight? And before you get excited about going back to Dewey's or to Graham for Italian or whatever, I have to tell you it's at my parents' house."

"I can't."

"I know you're not a big fan, but—"

"No, I mean I can't because I'm babysitting. Jennifer and Tommy are attending Hailey's program at church and I'm watching Tommy Jr. at their house. He's sick and can't go."

"Oh." Wyatt looked floored.

"I'm sorry. I probably would have come. I suppose, that is, unless your mother wanted to talk me into or out of something, in which case I would have to consider carefully." She didn't need political or social pressure from the town's wealthiest family. Especially now that she and Wyatt were dating. That put a twist on things, at least until she decided if she was running for office again and if she and Wyatt had a future.

Mrs. McCall hadn't liked her much way back when, but Toni supposed she was now more respectable since she was mayor and a businesswoman. And who knew what Mrs. McCall was thinking? Maybe she'd theorized that if Wyatt was dating someone local, he'd be around a lot more.

"I guess I could see if she wants to reschedule."

"No, you should go. Spend some time with the folks. It's the holidays. I'm sure they'd love to see you."

"I guess," he said, sounding rather like a ten-year-old who had been forced to do something slightly unpleasant but necessary. "I already told her I'd come and bring you."

"Well, you should have checked with me first."

"I know that now. I just wasn't thinking that you'd have anything tonight."

"I'm not some supermodel who can fly off on a whim."

"I didn't say you were."

"I know, but I get the impression your circle of friends and your prospective dates aren't so tied down by obligations."

"Now who's making assumptions about whom?"

Toni sighed. "You're right. I make a lot of assumptions about your lifestyle, mostly because I don't understand it. Having lots of free time to go on adventures and attend big, exciting events is as alien to me as…as babysitting Tommy Jr. must seem to you."

"I can imagine doing that. Do you want me to come with you?"

"No! You're having dinner with your parents, remember?"

"Oh, yeah. Well, how about later? I could bring dessert."

"Oh, no. Jennifer already warned me not to have my boyfriend slip into the house after the munchkin went to sleep."

"That used to be a lot of fun," Wyatt said, putting his arm around her waist as she stopped to unlock her door.

"Exactly why Jennifer mentioned it." Toni smiled as she opened the door and they stepped inside. "She remembers how we both used to let you and Tommy come over when we shouldn't."

"*Shouldn't* is such a strong word," he said, pulling her close in the foyer of her office. "Let's just say that some stuffy old adults didn't want us to have any fun."

Before she could reply, he kissed her, pulling her tighter as he slanted his mouth over hers. She immediately responded, her arms around his neck, her fingers in his hair. She went from amused to aroused in two seconds flat. And Wyatt did, too. She felt him hard against her stomach as she wiggled closer. His hand moved lower on her bottom, holding her against him as he moaned.

"Ahem!"

The sound coming from Toni's office was like a splash of cold water. *Oh my God.* Someone else had seen them making out like teenagers, probably in the reflection of the mirror.

"Geesh, guys. Can you get a room?" Leo shouted from the depths of the office.

"What… What are you doing here?" Toni asked in response to Leo's disembodied voice.

"We have a two-o'clock meeting, remember? About the pressed tin ceiling repairs versus new beadboard?"

"Oh. Yes, yes, of course." Toni pulled away, flushed and unfulfilled. Wyatt appeared just as frustrated.

"Call me later," she whispered. "After your dinner. The church program shouldn't run too late."

He nodded, kissing her quickly before pulling his leather jacket together over the front of his jeans and stepping outside.

The door closed. Toni glanced at the mirror. She looked as if she'd been thoroughly kissed. She wondered if she could attribute her messy hair and bright pink cheeks to her appointment at the salon and the brisk winter breeze.

"Come on in, sis. I promise not to give you a lecture."

Good. Because she didn't need one. She'd already decided that she wasn't going to let herself fall in love with Wyatt again. That didn't mean she might not fall into bed with him, however.

Chapter Fourteen

"I'm so sorry Toni couldn't come tonight," Wyatt's mother said as she handed him a casserole dish.

"Why the sudden interest in Toni? I got the impression you didn't see her all that much."

"Yes, but you're going out with her, aren't you? That's certainly of interest to us as well as others."

"Whether Toni and I are dating or not is our business."

"She's a public figure, so of course people are interested."

"What about you, Mom? What's the real reason you wanted me to bring her to dinner tonight?"

She sighed. "Well, you know we weren't in favor of you getting too serious about her when you were in high school. Your lives are much different now. She's grown into an accomplished young woman, and you are, of course, successful and established." His mother put a silver wire basket of crescent rolls on the table. "And neither you nor Toni are getting any younger. Maybe it's time."

"Time for what?" he asked, although he thought he knew where this conversation was going.

"Settle down, get married. Have a family."

"Oh, so I come back to town and you're already planning a nursery?"

"I'm not planning, just…hopeful."

"I'm not sure where our relationship is heading. Right now, we're dating." Good old-fashioned dating, which meant lots of tossing and turning at night, lots of sexual frustration. If someone had told him that he'd be in a kissing-only affair at age thirty-three, he would have told them they were nuts. And yet, here he was...

"We like Toni, son," his father said. "She's not one of those Hollywood types. Or a gold digger. She's a down-home Texas girl that you can trust."

"I know how trustworthy she is. I also know how important that is in a relationship. Still, anything beyond where we are right now is a big step, one that Toni and I will discuss first."

"We only want what's best for you," his mother said.

As opposed to all those years where you weren't real concerned with what was best, just what looked the best? But he tamped down his bitterness, since it wouldn't do any good to make snippy remarks. His parents were trying to do their jobs, finally, even if he didn't agree with their tactics.

"And your father and I are both getting older. We'd like to have grandchildren."

"That's one thing I can't buy for you," he said, the joke falling flat.

"We'd like to see you happily married first. I know that's not always the custom nowadays, especially out there in California, but—"

"If anything happens of a permanent nature, I'll let you know. For now, I'd appreciate it if you wouldn't try to influence Toni. We're getting to know each other as adults, not as kids, and we need the time to do that without interference."

"Of course we won't interfere. Will we, Margaret?"

"No, we won't," she said.

Well, at least Dad had stood up to her a little. If his mother had free rein, she'd probably be planning an engagement party for next weekend.

Engagement. Even the word evoked images of long, contracted arrangements and stressful plans for The Big Event.
Maybe Toni wouldn't want to go through with that traditional
step. Maybe, if they decided they could make a life together,
they could just fly off someplace and get married.

But, no, he'd cheated her out of an engagement once, by
making her believe that they would have that Tommy-loves-
Jennifer happy-ever-after ending, then leaving for Stanford.
If he and Toni were going to make this work, he'd have to suck
it up and do a real engagement, with a proper, memorable
proposal and a ring she'd be proud to wear. They'd have to
go through all the steps of planning a really nice wedding right
here in Brody's Crossing, and then…then what?

Where would they live? How would they mesh their lives
together? He didn't know, and he suspected Toni didn't, either.

"THANK YOU SO MUCH FOR babysitting Tommy Jr.," Jennifer
said around eight-thirty that night, shrugging out of her coat.
"How is he doing?"

"Same as the last time you called," Toni said with a smile.
"He's a little congested, but sleeping fine. You were right not
to take him tonight. He's just not feeling up to being around
other kids or being on his best behavior in church." Toni
smiled at Hailey. "How was the program?"

"It was great," the twelve-year-old said with a big grin. "I
sang two songs and I got to hold a candle while the choir sang
'O Little Town of Bethlehem.' That's one of my favorite
Christmas carols."

"We had cookies and hot chocolate after the program, in
the activity building of the church," Jennifer added.

"We drove by the community center, too," Hailey said. "I
love the new decorations. I want to roll those big ornaments
around," she confessed, then quickly added, "but I know I can't."

"No, they're all staked to the ground, since they're lighted.

We can't have them rolling around in the wind or being shifted in case someone isn't so sensible," Toni said.

"Hailey, I know you're still excited, but it's time to get ready for bed," Jennifer reminded her daughter.

"Oh, okay," she said. "Good night, Miss Toni."

"Good night, Hailey, and Merry Christmas."

Hailey smiled and waved a little as she walked down the hallway, yawning. Her dark-blond curls bobbed with each step. A little over a year ago, she'd lost all her straight, long hair. Now it had grown back darker and curlier. But the most important thing was that she was healthy once again.

"I can't tell you how much I appreciate you staying with Tommy Jr. We had a great time with Hailey. It's so good to see her participating in things again."

"I was happy to. I mean that."

"Are you sure Wyatt McCall isn't hiding in a closet or under the bed?"

"No, he didn't come over. Actually, he was having dinner with his parents."

"Oh. Well, it was fun to remember the times we did smuggle our boyfriends in when we were supposed to be alone."

"Or just with each other," Toni added, smiling.

"Exactly. So, I know I can't pay you for babysitting, but maybe I could take you to lunch after Tommy Jr. gets back in school. We could even go down to Graham to the tearoom."

"I'd love to. Just call me and we'll set up a time. My schedule is a little unpredictable with this hotel project, but I can usually work in a lunch. As a matter of fact, I look forward to getting away from the all-boys atmosphere on the job site."

"Okay, then. It's a date."

"You bet." Toni hesitated just a moment, then hugged Jennifer. "I missed you," she whispered.

"I didn't realize how much I missed you, too."

"Hey, is this one of those mushy girl moments? Because

if it is, I'm going back out to the truck," Tommy said, coming through the back door.

"Kind of, but I'm leaving," Toni said, wiping her eyes. She patted Tommy's arm on the way to her jacket. "I kind of missed you, too, you big lug."

"Gee, thanks," he said, trying to rub his knuckles into her scalp, which he knew she hated.

Toni laughed as she put on her jacket and picked up her purse. "Have a good night. I hope Tommy Jr. gets better soon."

"Thank you," Jennifer said, leaning against Tommy as he put his arm around her. "I'll see you soon for lunch."

"Definitely." Toni walked out to her truck. *I want that,* she thought as she breathed in the crisp night air. *I want what they have. Love and joy, even through the bad times. Children. A family.*

Only with the right person, though. Tommy and Jennifer had obviously made a go of their marriage. But they had other classmates who hadn't. Brody's Crossing had its share of divorces and split ups.

Toni started the truck before pulling her cell phone from her purse. *Call me.* She sent the mental message to Wyatt as she imagined him finishing dinner with his parents. *For a good time, call Toni.* She'd never been a victim, but she remembered the silly, hurtful messages that had been written on restroom stalls about other girls. For a good time tonight, she hoped Wyatt called. The sooner, the better.

WYATT PUT HIS HAND OVER her mouth as she screamed, pulsing light behind her closed eyes and intense pleasure infusing her whole body. She didn't think it was the first time he'd had to quiet her, but her brain was so fuzzy and the night was so dark and she'd been so turned on by the time they got to his motel room that she wasn't sure.

She held him tight as he muffled his own pleasure against

her neck and the pillow beneath her head. Just like old times, only better. How many times had they been forced to be quiet, to slip around in the dark, to be together in the most intimate sense of the word?

Tonight, she hadn't exactly slunk into his room, but they'd been discreet. He'd picked her up in his SUV. She'd left her truck in her driveway and kept a light on in the kitchen. They'd been quiet coming into the room. There was a couple or a family next door; Toni had heard the muffled sound of the television earlier.

And then Wyatt had kissed her, and she'd forgotten where they were. Didn't care who was around. Couldn't even think clearly.

Fortunately, he'd been aware enough to keep her from screaming, which probably would have prompted a 911 call from the room next door and lots of sirens in the parking lot. *Thank you, Wyatt, for saving me from myself.*

"I have to move, but I don't want to," Wyatt murmured against her neck, sending a wave of goose bumps down her arms.

"That was…incredible," she whispered.

"You always were a master of understatement," he said, raising up on his forearms. "I'll be right back." Kissing her, he pulled away and rolled to his side. He breathed deeply, then groaned and sat on the side of the bed. She watched him walk into the bathroom, his skin bleached white by the light filtering through the silvery curtains.

Suddenly she felt cold and very alone. She was covered in a fine sheen of perspiration, his scent and hers mingled together, and yet he wasn't there, pressed against her, and she felt the loss nearly as much as if he'd walked out the motel-room door. She felt a premonition, as if she were watching him leave forever.

Hey, babe, it's been great, but I can't stay. I'm feeling itchy, you know? Time to get back to my real life. You didn't really expect me to stay in Brody's Crossing, did you?

Oh, God, she was in love with him. Deeply, fully and undoubtedly, when she'd told herself—no, she'd *promised* herself—she would *not* fall in love with Wyatt McCall again.

She rolled away to stare at the window, not the bathroom, and pulled the sheet and satin comforter over her. Shivering, she tried to make sense of this sudden change in her life. Just a few weeks ago, she'd been perfectly grounded in her business and her political career. She'd known what she wanted, where she wanted to go and what she needed to do to get there.

If she'd been a little lonely, well, that was the price she had to pay for being a public figure. And a businesswoman who couldn't get too close to employees or suppliers. She couldn't wear her heart on her sleeve. And if she had a difficult time meeting eligible bachelors, then that was worth it for the esteem of the people she cared about.

Now, she felt lost. Falling in love was supposed to feel wonderful, but she wasn't glowing with an inner fire. All she could think about was that Wyatt would leave her. Again. This time, as an adult, she wasn't sure she could handle the loss as well as she had as a teenager. Back then, she'd gone away to college. Gotten out of the town where everyone knew almost every detail of Wyatt's desertion. Had met new friends and immersed herself in studies.

She was stuck here, and since so many people knew she and Wyatt had been dating, when he left they would also know he'd left her again.

Poor Antonia Casale. Poor Toni. What had happened? I thought they were going to make it this time.

No, she couldn't stand to hear those comments or see the sympathy in their eyes.

"Hey, what's wrong?" he asked, sliding back into bed and pulling her close. He felt so good, toned and tight, smooth in some places, hairy-rough in others. His chest was warm against her cold back, and only then did she realize she was shivering despite the comforter. "Did I hear you sniffle? Are you crying?"

"No! No, I'm not crying. I guess I'm just…emotional. You know…aftermath and all that," she hedged.

"Oh, babe," he said, pulling her tight. "Don't cry."

"I'm not. I won't," she promised, knowing she'd violate that vow before morning's light.

"You were happy earlier."

"I know. You left me and I started thinking. And that's not a good thing. I need you here beside me, Wyatt. Don't go."

"I'm not going anywhere."

Not yet, she thought, *but you will.*

"Hold me," she whispered. "Warm me."

"I will." He wrapped his arms around her and pulled her flush against him. He rubbed his feet along her cold ones. "Do you want me to turn up the heat?"

"As in the thermostat?"

"Or whatever," he said, kissing her shoulder.

She was already in love with him. She was already here, worried about him leaving. They'd made love this time, not just had sex under the stars.

"I choose whatever," she whispered, and turned in his arms to kiss his lips and lose herself in his arms.

ON THURSDAY, WYATT TALKED TONI into having lunch with him at Dewey's. He got to the restaurant early to secure a private booth near the back, then sat with a glass of sweet tea to think about what had happened in the past two days. First, Leo had had the big brother talk with him, and then his parents had put pressure on him to settle down. And then, last night… He and Toni had only been apart since around four o'clock in the morning, but already he missed her like crazy.

What did that mean, exactly? Something had happened last

night, although he wasn't sure what. Her earlier eagerness to be with him, her enthusiastic response to his kisses, had turned him on like never before. They'd made love last night, that much he knew. Did that mean that he was *in love?* Or that she was? Or that they were in love together?

He didn't know. He had no experience—as a grown man—with being in love. In the past fifteen years, he'd never told a woman he loved her. He knew that he'd loved Toni when they were teenagers. He'd loved her enough to leave her. He didn't want to break her heart later, when she discovered he wasn't husband material. He was still convinced that the clean break after high school had been best for both of them.

But now… Now, he didn't have the excuse of being too young, of having too many challenges ahead of him. He could write his own schedule, create whatever life he wanted. He might even be able to overcome his innate aversion to the *M* word. A hazy vision was beginning to form, in which he and Toni made their relationship work. Maybe they could even provide those grandchildren his parents wanted, although he wouldn't bring children into the world just because the senior McCalls wanted them to fulfill their own needs.

But the idea of a blond-haired little girl or a darker-haired mischievous little boy made him smile. Or maybe the roles would be reversed, and they'd get a hell-raising daughter and a studious, serious son. That was okay, too.

"You're in a good mood," Toni said, sliding into the booth across from him.

"You should come and sit by me, and I'll let you know what I was thinking about."

"I have a very good idea what you're thinking about, Wyatt McCall, and I'm not going to risk sitting by you while you try to talk me into anything."

"Would I do that?"

"Of course you would." Toni frowned. "Although, I have to admit, lately you've really been behaving yourself. Sometimes I think aliens have swooped down and replaced you with a kinder, gentler version of yourself."

"Hey, I was always kind."

Toni smiled. "That's true. In any case, you've been a perfect gentleman *in public,* and for that I thank you."

"I can be good," he said, giving her an exaggerated leer.

"Oh, you're very good," she said in a husky voice. "But don't get me started on that."

Wyatt chuckled. "Okay, your time is limited, so let's order. I have something else I want to discuss." He motioned for the waitress to come over.

"Hi, Twila," Toni greeted her. "I'll have the chicken tenders salad with ranch, and iced tea."

"I'll take the same," Wyatt said, handing back the menus.

"You've got it."

As soon as they were alone, Wyatt asked, "I'd like to plan something this weekend for the two of us, but I wasn't sure if you could get away."

"A whole weekend would be tough. George Russell is having his annual party, where he invites the city council, city manager, police chief and everyone else he deems important, on Saturday night, and then on Sunday afternoon we have the VFW Christmas party."

"Hmm, more obligations. Okay, how about Friday night?"

"I don't think I have anything then, although I usually have dinner with my folks and Leo."

"Will you come to Granbury with me? I reserved a room at a bed-and-breakfast there. I know you used to talk about visiting one of those, but we were too young at the time to pass ourselves off as a…well, you know. A couple."

Toni fidgeted with her napkin, folding it into a precise triangle. "Yes, I know. A married couple is what you're trying to say. And you're right. We couldn't have pulled that off way back then."

"Now I understand they're not so rigid."

"I suppose." She seemed withdrawn suddenly, as if talking about the past had upset her.

"If you'd rather not, I understand."

"No, I think it's a nice idea. We might as well do whatever we can while you're here, and during the Christmas holidays I don't have as many city council or department demands."

"I told you I wasn't going anywhere. At least, not for a while and not for long."

"You certainly can't live in the Sweet Dreams Motel forever, Wyatt. You have a home in California. You have your foundation, which I assume is important to you."

"It is! And I have been working on it. We're in a situation right now where I'm waiting for all the permits to be approved, all the leases to be signed. My assistant is taking care of most of that in California, but I'm online for conferences regularly. The whole point of the foundation is so that kids realize they don't have to act out to get noticed and they don't have to do something potentially harmful because they're bored. There are lots of smart kids who waste their potential because they don't have anyone who understands them."

"I'm sorry. I didn't mean that I was questioning your motives or your commitment to the kids. I think what you're doing is great. I'm just saying that your situation here seems temporary."

He sighed. What could he say? Toni was right about the facts, but she was still expecting him to get bored and leave. "I can guarantee that I won't get tired of you or the town."

"Okay. I'm just saying—"

"Just say that you want to go to the bed-and-breakfast with me. I think we'll have a good time. You deserve to get away. We can play tourist. Stroll around the town square, shop for antiques I don't like and you probably don't need, and eat in those froufrou places women like."

Toni smiled, then laughed. "Okay, since you've made your request so charmingly, how can I refuse? What time do I need to be ready tomorrow?"

"As early as possible in the afternoon." This afternoon, he had plans to do some more shopping for something special in Dallas.

TONI HAD A WONDERFUL TIME in Granbury, even though the four-poster canopy bed was a little short for Wyatt and the tiny sink in the bathroom was hard to negotiate when two people were getting ready at the same time.

They strolled the festive streets of the town square after a breakfast of quiche, sweet rolls and warm fruit compote. They went into almost every shop, and Toni found several Christmas gifts, including something for Jennifer, Hailey and Tommy Jr. As they were debating where to have lunch, Wyatt got a call from James. His friend and Sandy wanted Wyatt and Toni to come out to the ranch that afternoon. Their Christmas presents had arrived and they were all thrilled. They wanted to have an ATV riding party.

"What do you think, babe? Do we have time before you have to get ready for the Russell party tonight?"

"We'd have to leave real soon to get back." The drive to Brody's Crossing would take a little more than an hour. Riding ATVs would mean being more adventurous than she'd been in years. She'd almost forgotten the excitement of heading up a hill or across a trail where you couldn't see the other side. It was much like being with Wyatt—you never knew where you would end up. Could she share some of his daredevil ways?

"If you want to stay and shop, I'll tell him no."

Toni felt a wave of love roll through her. Wyatt was genuinely considerate. Kind, as he'd reminded her. That didn't mean that he loved her or that they could be together forever.

She held Wyatt's arm and forced a smile. "No, I'd love to go out to the Brody ranch. Please, tell James that would be great."

They finished looking through a couple of shops on the street on their way back to his SUV. Wyatt bought her a wide-brimmed feather-adorned red hat that he said she needed for next year's Settlers' Stroll. She didn't have the heart to tell him that was the type of hat worn by the ladies who met in restaurants and tearooms designed for the over-fifty club. He also found a yellow-striped cat Christmas ornament. For her tree, he told her, because that's what his cat back in Carmel looked like, only the real Tiger was a lot rougher-looking. Wyatt was sure that she'd like his cat, although Toni didn't understand how she would ever meet the feline, since they lived half a continent apart.

Knowing Wyatt, he'd probably charter a jet to bring the cat to Texas, just to visit. Toni didn't have pets. She didn't have time, and besides, they tore up furniture and carpets. That's what her mother had always claimed when Toni had wanted to bring a kitten or puppy home.

"We'd better get on the road," she said as they exited the store with more bags in hand. The weather was beautiful, in the sixties with little wind. "It's a perfect day for riding."

Wyatt smiled as he looked into the bright blue sky, just a few fluffy white clouds drifting overhead. "On days like this, it seems as if nothing could ever go wrong."

Chapter Fifteen

Dressed in faded jeans, an old work jacket and leather gloves to protect her hands, Toni felt as unfashionable as possible as she climbed aboard one of the new ATVs Wyatt had bought. She hadn't ridden one of these since high school, and she was sure it would feel odd to go tearing up the hill to the small mesa on the Brody ranch.

Wyatt and James had taken a steep route and made it near the top. Sandy had stayed lower. Toni was taking another route, also not as steep.

Limestone shards and fossils decorated the clay soil of the entire hill. While some stunted mesquite trees grew near the base, only a few bushes and some prickly pear cactus hung on the slopes. A few larger rocks poked through the dirt.

"I'm not going very far up," she told the group. "Don't try to goad me into more."

"You do whatever you want," James said.

"It's fun, but I didn't go too high, either," Sandy added.

"Come on, babe," Wyatt said near her ear. "Go for it."

She frowned at him. "Easy for you to say. You're an adventurer. The most exciting thing I do in a normal week is tear out drywall."

"Here's your chance, then. It's safer than skydiving or windsurfing."

"Two other activities I'm not trying."

Wyatt laughed. "Okay, I get the picture. Wussy girl."

She pointed her finger at him. "Don't start on me, Wild Wyatt McCall. I know your reputation."

They all laughed. The bantering reminded Toni of when she, Wyatt and James had been in high school. He'd been so polite and gentlemanly lately that he had hardly seemed like the old Wyatt. This was what she remembered…and loved.

Toni pulled down her safety goggles, shimmied on the seat until she felt she was in the right position, eased off the brakes and turned up the throttle. The vehicle took off, so she rolled back the gas a little, then surged forward again at a better rate. There, much smoother. She started going up the hill, which seemed steeper than when she'd looked at it from below. Rocks and pebbles flew from the rear tires. She heard the machine scrambling for purchase on the shifting soil and turned the wheel slightly for a better angle.

"That's it, babe! Go for it!" she heard Wyatt yell from below.

She felt an exhilarating lift when she realized she was gaining ground. The slope's angle changed, and she gave the ATV more gas. It leaped forward about the same time the front wheel hit a large rock that was partially covered in limestone shale. Rocks flew everywhere and the wheel started to slip. Toni tried to compensate, but she couldn't get it straight. The wheels continued to spin, propelling her sideways.

"Toni, use the front brakes," she heard Wyatt yell. "Don't let it flip!"

She couldn't get the ATV straight; she could only fall sideways. The last thing she saw before the bike went out from under her was a prickly pear bush in her downward path, and the last thing she did was try to jump clear of the needles. *This is going to hurt,* she told herself as she hit the ground and rolled. And rolled.

"I'M FINE," TONI SAID, swatting away the nurse's hand as she dabbed at a cut on her knee. Her ripped jeans had been cut away and thrown on the floor in the corner. They were spotted with blood. Every time Wyatt saw them, he nearly lost his lunch.

Toni sat on an exam table in the emergency room. She wore a pale blue printed hospital gown and an irritated expression. Her left wrist was covered in a brace, since it was sprained. She'd been given a painkiller, so Wyatt knew she wasn't suffering a great deal from her injuries, but she would as soon as the drug wore off. She'd feel terrible, and it was all his fault.

He shouldn't have insisted they ride the ATVs. Hell, he probably shouldn't have bought them. He definitely shouldn't have teased her into trying to make it up the mesa. He'd been irresponsible, as usual, and now Toni, the one woman he couldn't stand to see suffer, was covered with cuts and bruises. Not to mention regret and probably anger.

"I'm so sorry," he said when the nurse quit dabbing Toni's scrapes and left. "I didn't mean to hurt you."

"You didn't hurt me. I fell off the ATV."

"It's my fault," he said. "It was my gift, my idea. Now you're all banged up and you're supposed to be at a Christmas party tonight."

"Oh, well. This will give me an excuse to get out of going to the Russells' Christmas party," she said with a breezy wave of her good hand.

"You could have been hurt far worse."

"Yeah, but I'm tough."

She's loopy, he thought as he watched her unfocused brown eyes, bright cheeks and restless movements. *She doesn't realize the danger she was in.*

When he'd realized she was sliding off the ATV, then going over, he'd run, his heart nearly ready to explode. When she'd started up that hill, he'd urged her on, told her to go for it.

Called her a wussy girl. And here she was in a hospital gown, battered and bruised, her wrist sprained.

"You could have died," he said softly.

"Oh, don't be silly. I've fallen off ladders and through subfloors before. I've never died."

Sandy Brody stepped forward. "Wyatt, she'll be okay. Don't beat yourself up."

He shook his head. "It's my fault. She knows what a daredevil I was. I am. She was trying to keep up, trying to show me she's tough. I know she's tough."

"Hey, where's my juice?" Toni called out, her words slightly slurred.

Sandy found the cup of juice and held the straw up to Toni's lips. Her beautiful lips, which Wyatt had kissed in the early morning hours at the bed-and-breakfast, the sun filtering through the lacy curtains. She'd looked so peaceful and happy lying in the canopy bed, her pale skin unblemished and luminous.

He'd planned something far different for this afternoon, but then he'd gotten the phone call from James and all he'd thought about was how much fun it would be to go ride the ATVs on the ranch, just like old times.

He was an irresponsible fool. Risking his own life was one thing, but putting Toni in jeopardy was inexcusable. Unforgivable.

The doctor came into the room.

"Hiya, Doc," Toni said with a grin.

"Someone is enjoying her meds," the doctor said, taking a look at Toni's pupils. "I won't even ask you how you're feeling, because you probably don't know."

She waved her good arm again. "I'm fine. I keep telling him—" she pointed at Wyatt "—that I'm fine, but he won't believe me. Tell him, Doc."

"She needs bed rest until the hydrocodone wears off. Some people have this reaction. She should be fine in four or five hours. After that, I'll give you a prescription for Tylenol. She shouldn't have such a reaction to that."

"This stuff is good," Toni said. "Where's my juice?"

"Are you her husband?" the doctor asked.

"No." Wyatt took a small step back. "No." *I'm the jerk who caused the accident.* "We've been…dating."

"What's that mean?" Toni said. "We're dating now. This was a date, wasn't it?" She grabbed the doctor's sleeve and tugged. "We went to Granbury last night and stayed at a bed-and-breakfast. We had a *really* good time," Toni said with a wink.

"Okay, too much information," Sandy said, handing Toni the cup of juice again. "Here, sip."

Wyatt felt his head ready to explode. This wasn't happening. Toni wasn't injured and she wasn't loopy and telling the doctor that they'd done the wild thing at a B and B. That feeling came over him, the one where he had to do something or else. Itchy. He had the urge to run.

"I'll give some general instructions," he heard the doctor say to Sandy. "She has a slight concussion, so she'll have a headache. Keep her awake until tonight. She'll be sore after the painkiller wears off, but she'll be fine in a few days."

This time, Wyatt thought. What about next time? The next time he did something stupid?

"You behave yourself, young lady," the doctor told Toni, and Wyatt wondered why the doctor wasn't scolding him to behave himself. He was the one who'd screwed up. The doctor left to the sound of Toni's giggles.

I can't stay here, Wyatt thought. "James, can you and Sandy take Toni home? No, not home. To her parents' house. Take her there. They'll take care of her."

"Where are you going?"

"I… I have to leave. Something's come up." He'd driven Toni to the hospital in Graham in his rented SUV, and James and Sandy had followed in James's car. Fortunately, not

Sandy's little sports car. "Would you please have someone pack up my things and send them later? Um, check all the drawers. I'll pay, of course."

"Where are you going?" Toni asked, her voice revealing disbelief and hurt. "Can I go, too?"

Wyatt forced himself to step to the exam table and take her one good hand in his. He looked into her wide, slightly unfocused eyes. "I have to go, babe. I'm not good for you. I... I screwed up. I hurt you."

"No! You keep saying that. I was just rusty. Come on, we'll try it again! I'll bet I can make it up the hill this time. I'm not a wussy girl," she said, giggling.

Wyatt felt his skin shrinking, his head expanding. "No, Toni, you can't. I shouldn't have said that. I'm so sorry. I have to go, okay? Please, don't be mad at me. I didn't mean to hurt you."

"It's okay, Wyatt. Don't be sad," Toni said, squeezing his hand.

"You... You do what the doctor says, okay? You follow those directions and get better soon."

"Wyatt," she said, but he started to pull away. He had to leave. Now. He didn't want to shake off her grip. He just wanted to go away.

"Hey, Toni, how about some more juice," Sandy said, stepping between them, giving Wyatt a look that said she was disgusted with him. Toni finally let go of his hand.

The last thing he saw as he paused in the doorway was Toni's sad eyes, looking over Sandy's shoulder, silently asking him why he was leaving.

It's for your own good, babe. He walked as quickly as possible to the SUV and headed for the airport.

"I CAN'T BELIEVE HE'S GONE," Toni whispered as she stood in the doorway of the honeymoon suite of the Sweet Dreams Motel. The bed was made, the white Christmas tree's tiny lights blinked merrily from the dresser and a basket of baked goods sat on the cabinet that held a small refrigerator and microwave. His personal items were on the dresser, the nightstand, the bathroom countertop, as if he might return any moment.

Oh, God. Had he put away the condoms? Did everyone know that she and Wyatt had been here in his room, making love?

"He must have had an emergency," Christie said, pocketing the master keys.

"Something like that." Emergency-room panic attack. Emergency itchiness. Whatever you called it, he was gone. He'd taken the easy way out three days ago.

Toni had waited for him to return. To call. Long after the painkiller had worn off, she'd felt numb. Her injuries were healing, but her heart was broken. Again. When she'd realized what had happened, what Wyatt had done and why, the feelings had come back in a rush.

He'd left her again. This time out of guilt. Before, out of fear. Fear that he wasn't able to commit, that he wasn't "husband material."

"Um, do you want some time alone?"

"I guess so."

"If you'd rather not, I'll have the manager pack up his things. You don't have to—"

"No, I want to. He left because of me and I need to do this." She did. That didn't mean it would be easy.

"Don't try to lift anything with your wrist," Christie reminded her, pointing at her brace.

"I won't. I'll roll the suitcase, and I'll let you help me into the car with it."

"Okay, then. Just let me know when you're finished." Christie left. Toni imagined that her friend and business partner understood, or at least suspected, far more than she'd ever reveal about Toni's relationship with Wyatt.

With a sigh, Toni walked to the open closet and retrieved

the suitcase. Wyatt had obviously unpacked everything, which meant all his personal items were in the drawers. She had a lot of packing to do.

Touching his things was harder than she'd imagined. She remembered so much. He'd worn the cable-knit fisherman's sweater when he'd come to the office the day after the stage-coach abduction. She found the jeans he'd worn on their first real date, the cowboy boots he favored and the bandanna he'd used as a disguise the night he returned.

She folded each item and placed them all in his suitcase. She then went into the bathroom and packed his toiletries into a leather kit that, thankfully, concealed the condoms they hadn't used the other night. She found his shampoo and shaving cream, even his deodorant and toothpaste. Unscrewing the lid of his aftershave, she took a sniff and remembered how he smelled when she buried her head in the crook of his neck.

"God, this is hard," she said, clutching the bottle to her chest. She wanted him here, where they could hash out all their problems. Work through their issues. Make a decision together about whether she'd run for mayor again or where they might live if their relationship continued. Decide on a vacation spot they could visit together, someplace that wasn't too adventurous but would be interesting for both of them.

Surely they could compromise. Surely they could solve any problems if they just tried. But, no, he'd run instead of trying. He didn't have the guts to face her.

Why was he like this? She didn't know, and damn it, she couldn't very well ask him when he was all the way out on the West Coast, sitting in his big house with his cat and his house-keeper and his infinity pool overlooking the Pacific Ocean.

She knew he was there because she'd called Cassie to ask where to send his personal items.

By the time she got to the nightstand, she was so angry that she was stuffing things into his suitcase as quickly as possible.

The only item in the nightstand drawer was an unmistakable square blue box. Was it even his? What was this Tiffany box doing in Wyatt's room? But then she remembered he'd gone Christmas shopping one day. Maybe he'd bought this for his mother. Maybe he'd ordered it for her.

She was just about to put it in the suitcase when she remembered that you weren't supposed to pack expensive items, because sometimes the bags had to be inspected and—rarely—an unscrupulous baggage handler took things out of luggage. She'd lost a camera once that way.

Just a peek. She'd see what Wyatt had bought at Tiffany for someone, probably his mother, for Christmas. She opened the outside box, then the inside lid. A ring. Her heart began to beat fast. An engagement ring.

A huge diamond engagement ring. "Oh my God," Toni whispered. What was this? Was it what she thought? No, she shouldn't think that. She lifted the ring from its white velvet cushion and held it to the light. The diamond absolutely glowed. The facets created dozens of tiny rainbows. The setting was so beautiful it took her breath away.

As she tilted it back and forth to catch the light, she noticed the engraving on the inside. Feeling like a complete voyeur, she pulled it closer and read aloud, "'Toni, only 15 years late. Love, Wyatt.'"

Tears filled her eyes. "Damn you, Wyatt McCall. How dare you buy me this ring and run off to California?"

WYATT PUT HIS FEET UP ON THE end table, leaning back in the chair and watching the sun set from his balcony. Tiger sat on the wide arm, letting Wyatt stroke his back and giving him a rough purr as if he were bestowing a gift on humanity.

Below, the surf beat against the shore and the waves were tipped with pink. High clouds coming in from the northwest streaked the sky with purple, coral and yellow. This was one of those picture-perfect California days, but he didn't feel the joy or the peace. He didn't feel the Christmas spirit, not like he'd experienced it in Brody's Crossing.

He felt empty. Sometimes, when he had time to think, he wondered what had come over him when he'd looked at Toni in the emergency room. But then he remembered. He wasn't good for her. He'd been on his best behavior for several days and they'd had good dates. She'd even come to his room. Then he'd jumped at the chance to ride ATVs when he should have been proposing. When he'd finally decided he could take the plunge and get married, because that was the only way he could have Toni in his life forever.

And instead of getting a ring, she'd gotten a concussion, a sprained wrist, a dozen bruises and cuts. His heart had just about stopped when he'd seen her come off that seat, when she'd hit the rocks and rolled lifelessly down the hill.

He put a hand over his eyes and tried to rub away the image of Toni holding her wrist as he drove her to the emergency room in Graham. She'd told him even before the painkiller that she didn't blame him, that she wasn't mad at him, but she was far too forgiving. He'd screwed up and she'd see that sooner or later.

"Mr. McCall? You have a visitor," Mrs. Nakimoto said from the door to the balcony.

"A visitor? Not Brian or Cassie?"

"No. A lady. She said she must see you now."

"Is she waving a gun or a machete?"

"No, sir. She is a pretty lady, but not dressed as your other ladies dress. And she has a suitcase."

A suitcase. Surely… No, everyone traveled with a suitcase. That just meant this lady was not from around here.

"Okay, I'll come inside." The sun was almost set anyway. Darkness descended slowly, even on these shorter days. "Come on, Tiger," he said as he pushed out of the chair.

His cat hissed at him and twitched his tail. "Or stay here," Wyatt muttered.

He entered the clean, open living area of his house. Mrs. Nakimoto had not turned on many lights, knowing he didn't like a blazing-white interior, especially while the sun was still setting. He didn't see anyone at first, then he heard the whish-whish-bump of suitcase wheels across the big tiles.

She came into view. Toni, dressed in jeans and a loose cardigan sweater over a T-shirt, with sneakers on her feet. Her hair appeared slightly disheveled or windblown. And she was pulling his suitcase.

"When I asked someone to pack up my things, I didn't mean I expected them to be delivered personally," he said, walking toward her. His heart raced and he focused every bit of energy on remaining calm. Detached. "What the hell are you doing here? You should be home resting."

"I'm fine, you big jerk," she said angrily, coming to a stop. "I maxed out my credit card with a last-minute ticket purchase. I just spent all day at the airport and on a plane, much of that time sitting on the ground waiting to take off, to bring you this suitcase—" she fished around in her sweater pocket "—and this."

She smacked the blue box into his chest. Oh, yeah. That. What did you say to the woman you'd jilted twice? To the woman who had obviously read the engraving on the ring he'd hoped she'd wear forever?

"Well, do you have anything to say?"

"I… I don't know what to say."

"Did you mean it? That you loved me? That you were intending to ask me to marry you?"

"Yeah, I did." Last week. A lifetime ago. "Before I screwed up."

"Screwed up by leaving Brody's Crossing?"

"No! Screwed up by getting you on that ATV and then

taunting you into riding up that hill. You say you weren't seriously hurt, but the point is you could have been, and I would have been responsible."

"Do you honestly think that I'm so feebleminded that I make decisions based solely on whether you taunt me or not? How dare you imply that I'm that stupid!" She clenched her hands into fists and started pacing. "I'm not some weak-minded fool, Wyatt. Believe it or not, I make decisions every day without your input, and if you gave me advice on my business and I didn't agree with you, I'd tell you so and ignore it."

"This is different. You told me once that you couldn't think when I was around, or something like that."

"I wasn't talking about when you were around me like in public or the same county! I meant…intimate. You know what I mean," she said, waving her arms, then immediately winced.

"Please, don't hurt yourself."

"It was my choice to do something stupid, Wyatt."

"It's still my fault. We shouldn't have gone riding. I was going to propose to you that night, when we got back from Granbury. I had it planned. Nothing spectacular, because I was trying to be ordinary. Just a nice dinner and the ring. But, no, I had to jump at the chance to go ride ATVs with James. What does that tell you about me?"

"That you were practicing avoidance, the desire to put off what we aren't comfortable doing. That's all that means."

He felt stunned. She was turning everything around, making it seem simple when it wasn't. He'd put her in danger because he… Why? Had he ever thought about the danger? No, he'd only thought about the fun.

Because it was easier to have fun than to make permanent commitments.

He looked down at the ring box. When he'd chosen ATV riding over proposing, he'd been thinking only of himself. Selfish, just as he'd accused his mother of being selfish. She drank. He had adventures. Both were unfulfilling. Both were self-centered.

Why had he never seen that before?

"Okay, you figure this out," Toni said, standing maybe five feet away. "I don't know how we would have made everything work. You live here, I live there. You like to travel, I have responsibilities. I love my family, and you barely tolerate yours. But I do know that I love you, Wyatt McCall, and if you come to your senses you know where I'll be."

She started for the door.

"No, Toni, wait!"

Chapter Sixteen

"This is the craziest thing you've ever done," Leo complained as he climbed the metal ladder behind Toni. "I can't believe I went along with this."

"Be quiet, little brother, and carry the paint." Toni's progress was slow because of her sprained wrist, but she was determined to make it to the top. Just as determined were her brother and best friend. Determined to help, even though they thought she was nuttier than Myra Hammer's fruitcake.

"He's right," Jennifer said from farther down the ladder. "What if he—"

"Don't even say it!" Toni said quickly. If you didn't put your fears into words, they seemed a lot less scary. And right now, taking this step was stupid and silly and reckless and maybe even criminal. But when she'd walked out on him in Carmel, angry and hurt and uncertain after her mad dash to get there, she'd known she had to do something dramatic.

"How do you know he's coming?" Jennifer asked.

"Cassie called me."

"Oh."

They climbed to the top of the metal walkway that circled the water tower. Toni looked up at the big fake wreath and the weathered red bow that hung from the top, giving the water tower a little taste of the Christmas season. Some city worker had been even higher up here fairly recently. The idea gave her a feeling of vertigo that made her good hand clench on the rail. She would never, ever become a rock climber, even if Wyatt asked her to go on one of his adventures.

"You'd think the city would have put a gate and a lock on this thing," Toni muttered. Especially earlier in the month, when they first knew that Wild Wyatt McCall was coming back to town to finish his sentence.

"They probably didn't think that the *mayor* was planning an act of vandalism," Leo said, placing the paint on the walkway next to her.

"It's only paint," Toni muttered. "It's not like it's permanent." Not like a marriage, surely.

"Wow, look at this view," Jennifer said. "It makes my head swim."

"You don't have to do this, you know," Toni said, putting her good hand on Jennifer's arm.

"Are you kidding? This is fun. We haven't done anything this crazy in…" Her face fell when she realized what she was about to say.

"Fifteen years, right? Since Wild Wyatt McCall left town?"

"Well, yeah."

"It's okay. I understand, and you're right. But just like desperate times call for desperate measures, crazy times call for crazy measures."

"Well, this qualifies," Leo said. "Where should I start?"

WYATT DROVE INTO BRODY'S Crossing and went directly to the motel. He'd called his parents to tell them he was coming to town, so they wouldn't hear it from someone else. They might have meddled a little to get him back together with Toni, but their intentions seemed to be good. And as an adult, he could see that his mother was really trying. Over the past week or so, his resentment had started to fade. They weren't perfect, but they did love him, and his mother had conquered a serious addiction, a disease, which was something that he'd never objectively considered before.

Maybe he really was growing up.

"Have you seen it?" the manager asked, handing him a key.

"What? No, I don't suppose so. What is *it?*"

The manager chuckled. "Just drive all the way out Elm Street. You can't miss it," she said with a chuckle and a shake of her head.

It was probably a new city Christmas tree or some more lawn decorations. Maybe he'd inspired someone to decorate like Christmas on steroids.

He unpacked as quickly as possible and went back out to the Hummer. He liked the big rented vehicle and he wasn't trying to be ordinary any longer. If Toni wanted ordinary, she'd have to settle for someone else.

She'd probably be safer, but maybe she wouldn't be as happy. She wouldn't be loved. He'd come to those conclusions and more in the two days since she'd left him in Carmel.

He drove to her office, but she wasn't there. As he walked back to the Hummer, he noticed that not many people were around town. It was oddly deserted for a Thursday afternoon.

Where was everyone? Were they out seeing *it?*

He remembered being told that the beauty shop was the place where everyone talked about everything. He pulled out of the parking spot and headed south to Clarissa's House of Style, past the lamppost-mounted tinsel candy canes he hadn't gotten around to replacing.

"Next year," he promised the windblown decorations. As far as he knew, they hadn't been donated by any person or group who might miss their departure from the Christmas landscape.

The only person working at the shop was Venetia. She held a lethal-looking can of hair spray and a wicked metal comb over the tight curls of a little old lady Wyatt didn't know.

"Why, look who's here," Venetia said. "We weren't sure you were coming back."

"I didn't know my return was of public interest."

"Oh, it is now," Venetia said, and chuckled.

"What does that mean?" He was getting slightly irritated by the smirking tone of these comments.

"You'll see. The only reason I'm here is that someone had to style Mirabelle's hair for her cousin's funeral in Decatur. Otherwise, I'd be with most everyone else in town."

"Is this where you tell me that I'm supposed to drive west on Elm Street?"

"That's right!"

"What am I looking for?"

"You'll know it—"

"—when I see it. Got it. One more question. Is there someone I could get more information from?"

"You should just drive out Elm Street. All your questions will be answered."

"Okay. Thanks, I guess. And sorry about your loss."

"Thank you kindly, young man," Mirabelle said. "Do I know him?" he heard her ask Venetia as he walked out the door.

He got into the Hummer and drove west on Main Street to the stoplight, then turned right on Commerce and left on Elm. He passed the police station on the corner and the neat houses along the residential street that reminded him of Toni's bungalow, just a block away. All the homes were decorated for the holidays, with Christmas just over a week away.

If she accepted his proposal, they'd need a bigger house. He had nothing against her place, but it wasn't spacious enough for his seventy-two-inch plasma TV, workout equipment and rock-climbing wall. He'd seen only a one-car garage, which didn't look as though it could be expanded to house his four vehicles and his motorcycles.

The sun was getting low in the sky as he passed the last

house and headed up the hill. He remembered the drive well. The last time he'd been here was a little more than two weeks ago, when he and Toni had made love under the stars. The time before that had been fifteen years earlier, when he and Toni had made love under the stars. Definitely a pattern was developing.

He shook away the memories and realized that there were cars lining the two-lane road. People waved at him and smiled. He frowned and waved back. What was going on? He felt like the only float in a one-man parade.

He turned the corner and looked up at the water tower he'd once painted purple and gold. Well, he and James, but he hadn't given his friend away. Now it was white again, decorated with a big wreath, and… What was that on the side? Black lettering? Was the town so desperate that they rented out advertising space?

He stopped the Hummer and looked. The sun shone in his eyes, so he got out for a better viewing angle. People in the cars around him started clapping. He felt as if he'd entered a surreal world.

"What's going on?" he asked everyone in general.

"Read it," someone shouted.

Shielding his eyes, he looked up. *You'll know it when you see it.* This must be it.

He tilted his head, the angle making the letters hard to read. *"M-A-R-R-Y,"* he spelled out. He walked a few steps and continued. *"M-E."* His heart sped up as he walked a few more steps. *"W-Y-A-T-T."* He stopped and stared. "Marry me, Wyatt." Then a big heart, and the word, *Toni*.

Toni? "Where is she?"

"Up there!" someone shouted.

He shielded his eyes again and looked. Sure enough, on the walkway around the water tower, Toni stood, her blond hair blowing in the breeze, her good arm waving. His heart skipped a couple of beats at the sight of her, high overhead.

He ran toward the tower, people cheering him on. "You're crazy," he shouted, but she shook her head, either denying the fact or unable to hear him.

"You're crazy," he shouted again as he reached the base and looked up.

She looked over the railing, down at him. "I love you," she shouted.

"I love you, too. Now, get down here before you break your other arm!"

She laughed and headed for the ladder.

"No! Wait! It's too dangerous."

Leo walked over, then Jennifer Wright. "She climbed up there," Leo said. "I think she can climb down."

"You were here? And you didn't stop her?"

"Hell, no. Have you ever tried to stop Toni from doing something she really wanted to do?"

"She was highly motivated," Jennifer said.

"She's highly insane," Wyatt said, watching her inch down the ladder. "She's wearing a cast!"

"No, just a brace," Leo said.

"Don't be mad at her. She did this in a big way, the best that she could," Jennifer said.

"She could have just said yes when I propose later."

"Yes, but this is one of those stories you can tell your grandkids someday."

Wyatt swallowed. Grandkids meant kids first. They hadn't talked about that. He'd been worried about where to put his gym equipment and he hadn't thought about a nursery.

Of course he wanted kids. With Toni. He didn't even mind that in doing so he'd make his parents happy. Maybe his mother would be a better grandmother than she'd been a mother. She was clean and sober, and she was enthusiastic.

Toni neared the bottom. He strode the few steps and caught her around the waist as she prepared to step off the ladder.

"That was the craziest thing you've ever done," he said as he swung her down. "Please don't ever make me worried about you again."

"I can't promise that," she said, running her hand around his jaw. "But I can promise that I'll love you forever."

He swept her into his arms and kissed her with all the passion and frustration and love he'd bottled up inside for days and weeks and years. He kissed her as if he'd never let her go.

When he did, finally, he realized that the people of Brody's Crossing had gathered around, and they were clapping.

"Well done, Toni!" someone yelled.

"Well done, Wyatt," someone else said.

He smiled down at Toni. Her hair was windblown and she was smudged with black paint, but she'd never looked more beautiful. "I really do love you, you know."

"I know. And I really do love you, too, even when you make me mad and get me all shook up."

"Okay, then." He dropped to one knee and pulled the ring box out of his pocket. "Antonia Casale, will you do me the honor of becoming my wife and my best friend, again, and this time forever?"

Tears sparkled in her eyes, reflecting the setting sun. "I will—if you'll take me as I am, where I am."

He placed the engagement ring on her finger and watched the stone pick up the pinks and yellows of the sky. "I'll live here for as long as you want, if you'll promise me you'll take time from your business every now and then. The sunsets are nice in Carmel, too, and Australia, and Alaska, and Peru, and—"

She put a finger to his lips. "I get the picture. Yes, I will live with you and travel with you as much as I can. But our home is here, in Brody's Crossing, among the people we love."

"Does that mean you're running for mayor again?" he asked.

"I think I owe them one more time."

"She said yes and she's running for mayor again!" Claude McCaskie shouted. A cheer went up from the crowd.

Wyatt smiled and looked around. Her parents were wiping their eyes; Leo and Jennifer were smiling and heading toward Toni. Wyatt saw so many people that he'd known all his life, so many friends and new friends. He felt as if he'd received the best Christmas present ever, the gift of his own sense of place in the world.

His place was, and always had been, with Toni. He just hadn't realized it until he'd almost lost her.

He would have to share her with the town, but that was okay, because at the end of the day, he knew right where she'd be. In his arms.

* * * * *

Silhouette Desire kicks off 2009 with
MAN OF THE MONTH, *a yearlong program*
featuring incredible heroes by stellar authors.

When Navy SEAL Hunter Cabot returns home for some
much-needed R & R, he discovers he's a married man.
There's just one problem: he's never met his "bride."

Enjoy this sneak peek at Maureen Child's
AN OFFICER AND A MILLIONAIRE.
Available January 2009 from Silhouette Desire.

One

Hunter Cabot, Navy SEAL, had a healing bullet wound in his side, thirty days' leave and, apparently, a wife he'd never met.

On the drive into his hometown of Springville, California, he stopped for gas at Charlie Evans's service station. That's where the trouble started.

"Hunter! Man, it's good to see you! Margie didn't tell us you were coming home."

"Margie?" Hunter leaned back against the front fender of his black pickup truck and winced as his side gave a small twinge of pain. Silently, then, he watched as the man he'd known since high school filled his tank.

Charlie grinned, shook his head and pumped gas. "Guess your wife was lookin' for a little 'alone' time with you, huh?"

"My—" Hunter couldn't even say the word. *Wife?* He didn't have a wife. "Look, Charlie…"

"Don't blame her, of course," his friend said with a wink as he finished up and put the gas cap back on. "You being gone all the time with the SEALs must be hard on the ol' love life."

He'd never had any complaints, Hunter thought, frowning at the man still talking a mile a minute. "What're you—"

"Bet Margie's anxious to see you. She told us all about that R & R trip you two took to Bali." Charlie's dark brown eyebrows lifted and wiggled.

"Charlie…"

"Hey, it's okay, you don't have to say a thing, man."

What the hell could he say? Hunter shook his head, paid for his gas and as he left, told himself Charlie was just losing it. Maybe the guy had been smelling gas fumes for too long.

But as it turned out, it wasn't just Charlie. Stopped at a red light on Main Street, Hunter glanced out his window to smile at Mrs. Harker, his second-grade teacher who was now at least a hundred years old. In the middle of the crosswalk, the old lady stopped and shouted, "Hunter Cabot, you've got yourself a wonderful wife. I hope you appreciate her."

Scowling now, he only nodded at the old woman—the only teacher who'd ever scared the crap out of him. What the hell was going on here? Was everyone but him nuts?

His temper beginning to boil, he put up with a few more comments about his "wife" on the drive through town before finally pulling into the wide, circular drive leading to the Cabot mansion. Hunter didn't have a clue what was going on, but he planned to get to the bottom of it. Fast.

He grabbed his duffel bag, stalked into the house and paid no attention to the housekeeper, who ran at him, fluttering both hands. "Mr. Hunter!"

"Sorry, Sophie," he called out over his shoulder as he took the stairs two at a time. "Need a shower, then we'll talk."

He marched down the long, carpeted hallway to the rooms that were always kept ready for him. In his suite, Hunter tossed the duffel down and stopped dead. The shower in his bathroom was running. His *wife?*

Anger and curiosity boiled in his gut, creating a churning mass that had him moving forward without even thinking about it. He opened the bathroom door to a wall of steam and the sound of a woman singing—off-key. Margie, no doubt.

Well, if she was his wife… Hunter walked across the room, yanked the shower door open and stared in at a curvy, naked, temptingly wet woman.

She whirled to face him, slapping her arms across her naked body while she gave a short, terrified scream.

Hunter smiled. "Hi, honey. I'm home."

* * * * *

Be sure to look for
AN OFFICER AND A MILLIONAIRE
by USA TODAY *bestselling author Maureen Child.*
Available January 2009 from Silhouette Desire.

CELEBRATE
60 YEARS
OF PURE READING PLEASURE
WITH **HARLEQUIN**®!

We'll be spotlighting a different series
every month throughout 2009
to celebrate our 60th anniversary.
Look for Silhouette Desire® in January!

MAN of the **MONTH**

Collect all 12 books in the Silhouette Desire®
Man of the Month continuity, starting in
January 2009 with *An Officer and a Millionaire*
by *USA TODAY* bestselling author
Maureen Child.

*Look for one new Man of the Month title
every month in 2009!*

REQUEST YOUR FREE BOOKS!
2 FREE NOVELS PLUS 2
FREE GIFTS!

Love, Home & Happiness!

YES! Please send me 2 FREE Harlequin® American Romance® novels and my 2 FREE gifts (gifts are worth about $10). After receiving them, if I don't wish to receive any more books, I can return the shipping statement marked "cancel." If I don't cancel, I will receive 4 brand-new novels every month and be billed just $4.24 per book in the U.S. or $4.99 per book in Canada. That's a savings of close to 15% off the cover price! It's quite a bargain! Shipping and handling is just 25¢ per book, along with any applicable taxes.* I understand that accepting the 2 free books and gifts places me under no obligation to buy anything. I can always return a shipment and cancel at any time. Even if I never buy another book from Harlequin, the two free books and gifts are mine to keep forever.

154 HDN EEZK 354 HDN EEZV

Name	(PLEASE PRINT)	
Address		Apt. #
City	State/Prov.	Zip/Postal Code

Signature (if under 18, a parent or guardian must sign)

Mail to the **Harlequin Reader Service:**
IN U.S.A.: P.O. Box 1867, Buffalo, NY 14240-1867
IN CANADA: P.O. Box 609, Fort Erie, Ontario L2A 5X3

Not valid to current subscribers of Harlequin® American Romance® books.

Want to try two free books from another line?
Call 1-800-873-8635 or visit www.morefreebooks.com.

* Terms and prices subject to change without notice. N.Y. residents add applicable sales tax. Canadian residents will be charged applicable provincial taxes and GST. Offer not valid in Quebec. This offer is limited to one order per household. All orders subject to approval. Credit or debit balances in a customer's account(s) may be offset by any other outstanding balance owed by or to the customer. Please allow 4 to 6 weeks for delivery. Offer available while quantities last.

Your Privacy: Harlequin is committed to protecting your privacy. Our Privacy Policy is available online at www.eHarlequin.com or upon request from the Reader Service. From time to time we make our lists of customers available to reputable third parties who may have a product or service of interest to you. If you would prefer we not share your name and address, please check here.

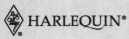

HARLEQUIN®

American ★ *Romance*®

TINA LEONARD
The Texas
Ranger's Twins

Men Made in America

The promise of a million dollars has lured
Texas Ranger Dane Morgan back to his family
ranch. But he can't be forced into marriage to
single mother of twin girls, Suzy Wintertone,
who is tempting as she is sweet—can he?

**Available January 2009
wherever books are sold.**

LOVE, HOME & HAPPINESS

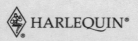

HARLEQUIN®

American ★ Romance®

COMING NEXT MONTH

#1241 THE TEXAS RANGER'S TWINS by Tina Leonard
Men Made in America
Texas Ranger Dane Morgan has been lured home to Union Junction by the
prospect of inheriting a million dollars. All he needs to do is live on the
Morgan ranch for a year...and marry Suzy Winterstone. While the sassy single
mother of toddler twin daughters is as tempting as she is sweet, no Ranger
worth his salt can be forced into marriage by a meddling matchmaker! *Can he?*

#1242 MILLION-DOLLAR NANNY by Jacqueline Diamond
Harmony Circle
When her con man ex-fiancé takes off with all her money, Sherry LaSalle finds
herself in need of something she's never had before—a job! The socialite may
have found her calling, though, as a nanny for Rafe Montoya's adorable twin niece
and nephew. The sexy mechanic couldn't be more different than the ex-heiress, but
there's something about Sherry that's winning over the kids...and melting Rafe's
heart.

#1243 BABY ON BOARD by Lisa Ruff
Baby To Be
Kate Stevens is interviewing daddy candidates. Applicants must be kind, must
be stable and must be looking for the same white-picket-fence life Kate has
always dreamed of. Unfortunately for her, fun-loving, risk-taking world traveler
Patrick Berzani—the baby's biological father—wants to be considered for the
position....

#1244 MOMMY IN TRAINING by Shelley Galloway
Motherhood
The arrival of a megastore in Crescent View, Texas, is horrible news for
Minnie Clark. Her small boutique is barely making a profit, plus she has
the added responsibility of providing for her young niece. So when Minnie
discovers that her high-school crush, Matt Madigan, works for the megastore,
the new mommy is ready for battle!